STEPMOTHER EARTH

Yakup Kadri Karaosmanoğlu

Translated by Mark David Wyers

Milet

Milet Publishing
Smallfields Cottage, Cox Green
Rudgwick, Horsham, West Sussex
RH12 3DE England
info@milet.com
www.milet.com
www.milet.co.uk

First English edition published by Milet Publishing in 2019

ISBN 978 1 78508 930 5

First published in Turkish as *Yaban* in 1932

Funded by the Turkish Ministry of Culture and Tourism TEDA Project

Printed and bound in Turkey by Yazın Matbaacılık

Yakup Kadri Karaosmanoğlu was born in Cairo in 1889, which at that time was part of a tributary state of the Ottoman Empire, but his family soon moved to the Turkish territories of the empire. He launched his literary career in 1909 when he became part of a progressive group dedicated to literature, many members of which would have a major impact on literature in the early years of the Republic of Turkey, which was founded in 1923 after the fall of the Ottoman Empire. He was a prolific writer, dedicating most of his writing to novels, poetry, and plays, and he was also an active journalist. In addition, he studied law. Because of his support for the Turkish War of Independence, in the 1920s he was summoned to Ankara, Turkey's capital, where he launched his political career, for which he travelled throughout the hinterlands of the young country. His travels in the rural areas of Anatolia played a key role in the writing of *Stepmother Earth*. Karaosmanoğlu, whose work is firmly established as part of the literary canon for the early years of the Republic of Turkey, died in Ankara in 1974.

Mark David Wyers was born in Los Angeles, California and received his BA in literature from the University of Tampa. He went on to live in Turkey in the cities of Kayseri, Ankara, and Istanbul, and later he completed an MA in Turkish studies at the University of Arizona. From 2008 to 2013 he worked as the director of the Writing Center at Kadir Has University in Istanbul, during which time he wrote a book-length historical study titled *"Wicked Istanbul": The Regulation of Prostitution in the Early Turkish Republic*, which drew upon his master's thesis. Inspired by the translations he was doing for his research, he began translating Turkish literature into English. He has translated numerous novels, including Selim İleri's *Boundless Solitude* and Feyza Hepçilingirler's *As the Red Carnation Fades*, which were published by Milet, and his translations of Turkish short stories have appeared in various journals, magazines, and anthologies, including *Istanbul in Women's Short Stories*, *Europe in Women's Short Stories from Turkey*, and *Aeolian Visions/Versions: Modern Classics and New Writing from Turkey*, which were also published by Milet.

Note on Turkish Terms

Some honorific titles have been retained from the Turkish in the translation. The ones that appear in this book are:

Ağa: A local large landowner; used after a man's given name, it is an honorific for local notables.
Efendi: A respectful term of address used to refer to or address a high-ranking individual.
Hanım: A respectful term of address used after a woman's given name.
Kadın: Literally "woman." In rural settings, a respectful term of address used after a woman's given name.

Guide to Turkish Pronunciation

Turkish letters that appear in the book and which may be unfamiliar are shown below, with a guide to their pronunciation.

c   as *j* in *just*
ç   as *ch* in *child*
ğ   silent letter that lengthens the preceding vowel
ı   as *a* in *along*
ö   as German *ö* in *Köln*, or French *œ* in *œuf*
ş   as *sh* in *ship*
ü   as German *ü* in *fünf*, or French *u* in *tu*

There is a brief glossary at the back of the book for terms that were retained in Turkish.

Note Concerning the Title

The original Turkish title of this work is *Yaban*, a word with Persian roots. As a noun, it means "desert" or "wilderness," while as an adjective it carries the meaning of "wild" or "savage." At the same time, however, it also connotes "the world of strangers" in the sense of outsiders who are not part of the family or local community. Yakup Kadri Karaosmanoğlu stated that he disapproved of the simplistic translation of "The Stranger" ("L'Étranger") for the reason that it did not accurately reflect the essence of the book, and he said he'd prefer for the title to remain untranslated. He did note, however, that of all the translations, he found the Italian title *Terra Matrigna* ("Stepmother Earth") which was published in 1941, to be the most fitting, so we decided to respect his wishes in that regard.

After the Battle of Sakarya, the enemy army left in its wake a vast, desolate wasteland. The districts of Haymana, Mihalıççık, and Sivrihisar, which lie to the south and southwest of Ankara, had been torched, and in some places little remained but smoldering heaps of embers. As they huddled half-clad among piles of rubble, the people who had survived the calamity were living in a state no different than the first humans who walked the earth. They tried to grind seared kernels of wheat and corn on threshing floors blackened by the fires and gnawed on the roots of trees and the leaves of weeds in their search for nourishment, and whenever they heard a stranger approaching, they fled in fear, cowering in hollows and caves.

The War Crimes Committee, which had been sent out by the command on the Western Front, was searching among those ruins for the burnt skeletons of civilians when it came upon a tattered, charred notebook, the contents of which are presented here. They asked the local villagers what happened to the man who had penned the notebook, but no one knew where he'd gone. All they said was that he'd lived in the village for a few years and that he vanished on the day of the calamity.

One of the members of the War Crimes Committee was particularly taken aback by their apathy.

"How is that possible?" he asked. "How could you not know what happened to someone who had been living among you for years?"

Shrugging irritably, the villagers started walking away.

But one of them, a short, thin man of indeterminate age, turned and said, "Well, he was a stranger like yourself."

For someone who had cut himself off from the world, what better place to retire from society than this remote corner of Anatolia? I feel as though I've been buried alive here. No act of suicide has ever been more intentional, resolute, drawn out, or difficult.

Suppose that, even before you reach the age of thirty-five, you confess to yourself that the game is up and there is nothing more to be done, and that love, passion, hope, and ardor have dried up, never to be stirred to life again; saying that all the doors to happiness and success have closed, you come to this place, condemning yourself to wither away like a dying tree. Is this how it was supposed to be? Is this what I'd been thinking? In the end, that's how it turned out, and it couldn't have been any other way.

When Mehmet Ali said to me, "Sir, allow me to take you to my village. Here you'll just suffer from loneliness," I wasn't unaware of what life is like in the villages of Anatolia.

When Mehmet Ali said to me, "Sir, allow me to take you to my village," I imagined precisely how this village would be, even Mehmet Ali's house, this room, and the view I see as I peer out from this tiny window . . . It matters little, for prior to losing my arm during the Great War I'd already lost all my poetic faculties as well as the ability to express myself plainly. Through "the blood on its fingertips and mud on its forehead," reality had appeared to me in its ghastliness, crudity, and vileness. I knew that the earth is hard and nature is cruel, and also that human beings are nothing more than degenerate animals. I also knew that people are the worst of animals, the basest and least likable. Yes, the least likable of them all.

Ever since I've been living here among the village's donkeys, water buffalo, goats, and chickens, I've come to see and understand that fact more clearly.

The honesty and candor of animals' simplicity, sincerity, and instincts make you overlook their faults. The instincts of humans, on the other hand, are depraved. That's why they cannot distinguish between right and wrong, beautiful and grotesque, or useful and useless, and under the sway of that hellish instrument we call the intellect, people go through life convulsing in the most preposterous, base, foolish, and tactless manner. For the same reason their actions are stilted, their voices grate on the ears, and their joy is coarse and short-lived.

I've seen it. All of civilized humanity paraded before my very eyes. The Racines and Voltaires of the French, the Bacons and Shakespeares of the English, the shrewd Italians, and the children of those who conquered the power of lightning, they all passed before me with their particular garb, colors, speech, and laughter. What an unschooled, vulgar, disgusting, monstrous troop of gorillas!

They're not even barbarians or predators. Whenever their cheeks bulged with everything they'd seized and they frolicked with one another, I'd be overcome by despair, spiritual anguish, and a deep sense of gloom.

Time and time again I longed to grab a stick and round them up so I could drive them back to their own woods, but I didn't have a right arm . . .

Isn't that the reason why they would sneer at me when I was in their midst and try to play with my right sleeve, which sways back and forth like an empty sack? One day I decided to fold up the cuff of my sleeve and tuck it into my pocket so it wouldn't swing around all the time, and that's what I've done ever since when I go out.

In this village, however, no one notices that I'm missing an arm, although I wish that they would because I lost it for their sake. What had been a mark of contempt in Istanbul became a badge of honor for me here. In the early days, when I would stroll around the village with Mehmet Ali, I'd always turn my right side towards the people we came across. In particular, I went out of my way to make the young men and women take note of the fact that I was maimed. It was my final adornment, so to speak, and my last point of flair. But within a week that fell away. Far from garnering their admiration, it didn't even stir up any feelings of compassion. Why, I wondered. Later I came to understand that it was because in the village, nearly everyone has their own particular infirmity.

Mehmet Ali's mother has a heavy limp. One of Salih Ağa's sons is hunchbacked. Zehra, the daughter of Bekir Çavuş, is blind. I haven't seen her for myself, but Mehmet Ali told me that the wife of the *muhtar* was stricken with an unknown disease eight years earlier that left her so badly bent over and contorted that her arms cannot be pried from her legs. There is only one part of her body that still shows any signs of life, and that's her eyes. They say that the muhtar shouts at her day in and day out, "What's done is done, so go on and die!"

Aside from them, the village has two crackpots and a midget. In such a place swarming with the afflicted and maimed, how would anyone ever take notice of me?

All the same, ever since my first day here the villagers have kept me at arm's length. An invisible barricade, a quarantine cordon fence of sorts, has kept me apart from that clan of people with whom I want to rub shoulders. No matter what I do, I can't seem to break through to them. So within this village, which itself is encircled by a horrific vast barrenness, I am hemmed in by yet another barrenness.

If not for Mehmet Ali, no one would talk to me, and they would keep a wary distance, eyeing me as if I was a scarecrow that had been erected on the street. At first, children would scatter in terror when I drew near and dogs would trail along behind me, barking wildly. But I am neither strange, nor frightening. To the contrary . . . I came here to escape being among strangers, to escape the malice of strangers. What I wanted was to spend time with this small clan of people who, I thought, were my kinsmen, to mingle with them and cast off my desolation. On the trip to the village, I kept saying to Mehmet Ali:

"Your mother will be my mother and your siblings will be my siblings. I want you to know that." And without answering, his swarthy face would broaden into a child-like grin.

Was he silently smiling because he knew that would be impossible? Who knows . . . The souls of Turkish villagers are still, deep waters. What lies at the bottom? Craggy boulders, mounds of sludge, smooth sand? We'll never know, as those depths cannot be plunged.

When I speak to them, they gawk at me as if they don't understand, and then they start murmuring to one another. I get the feeling that in fact they do understand but disapprove of the things I say. Sometimes it seems like they are laughing up their sleeves.

In my first few weeks in the village, my presence spread nothing but fear and suspicion. I'm not sure if they thought I'd been sent by the government as a civil servant, taxman, tithe collector, gendarme, or head of some military outpost, but I could clearly see the trepidation and distrust in the expressions of everyone I came across.

Over time they came to understand that I was none of the above but rather a mere nobody, and those foreheads wrinkled by fright gave way to looks of consternation and sly sneers. At the time I discerned in their eyes an odd bead of light that seemed to pulse, glowing brighter and fading, fading and glowing brighter. I can't remember ever seeing anything that made me feel as uneasy as that bead of light, which I was certain was the emanation of some obscure, diabolical intelligence the source of which is so distant as to be inaccessible for me. Its gaze observes me incessantly everywhere I go, even penetrating into my room, which is my only sanctuary, never giving me a moment of respite, not even when I'm getting undressed, bathing, or shaving.

My most basic, natural actions are as bizarre to them as would be the somersaults, leaps, and tumbles of a clown in a circus.

I asked Mehmet Ali, "Why does everything about me seem so strange to the people in your village?"

At first, he tried to deny that anything was amiss, but then, unable to restrain himself, he started dropping me pearls of advice, one by one:

"Sir, leave off shaving every day."

"Sir, out here in the sticks you don't need to brush your teeth morning and night."

"Sir, around here only women comb their hair."

"Sir, you always sit up at night and read till dawn. If you go on doing that, they'll think you're doing magic."

What am I supposed to do if I *don't* read until dawn? In the evening when everyone has retired to their homes, I can't wait to bolt my door and be alone with my books, because that is the only time I can forget about all of the mournful travails of this life and the torments of the moment that weigh on me. Those are the hours when this bare, austere room begins to fill with delightful, amiable beings, every one of them imbued with magic, beings from another realm that is vaster and more gladsome than the real world.

Rare beauties whose scent lingers in the air after they've gone, friends whose voices are tenderer and dearer than those of a mother, men and women with limpid eyes that glimmer like plashing brooks such as Dante's Beatrice, Petrarch's Leonora, Romeos and Juliets, and many more charming phantoms . . . Some sit side by side on the bed, while others curl up in my lap like a small child; some sit alone in the armchair, and others merely stand; some gaze outside with their elbows on the windowsill, and others pace around the room until dawn; and when day breaks and the sound of a divine orchestra reverberates through the air, the creators join hands with their creations as they all sway to the sound of the music.

*

It was dusk when we first arrived. His arm extended out the open window of the carriage, Mehmet Ali pointed and exclaimed:

"There it is, my village!"

I peered into the gloom. Initially, I didn't see anything, but a while later I thought I could make out something shadowy in the distance. There wasn't a single light. All I could hear was the barking of dogs, and that sound was the only sign of life on these central Anatolian plains. Still, I surmised that soon enough I would breathe in the smell of hay and cow dung, and that's precisely what happened.

Mehmet Ali, who was now leaning halfway out of the carriage in the direction of the village, had lost all interest in our conversation, and I hoped that he wouldn't forget about me altogether when we arrived. Even then, a feeling of resentment against him was welling up within me. It was as if I was jealous of that village of his. Perhaps it would be more correct to say that I felt my very presence was an intrusion on that private from the army who was returning home after four years. I couldn't help but ask myself: What am I doing here? Why did I send myself off to this province of exile?

Province of exile? How could these lands, as part of this fair country where not a single enemy soldier has set foot, be a province of exile? No matter how much I may come to deny it, I cannot hide my feelings on the issue: As we drew nearer to Mehmet Ali's village, I started getting the feeling that I had left something behind, something sacred. A heaviness weighed on my heart.

What, however, could I have left behind that would bring on such a sense of melancholy? A home? A mother? A lover? No. No one, nothing.

I was going there to find all that I'd lost.

The carriage clattered to a shuddering halt as if it had struck a large stone in the road. Without saying a word, Mehmet Ali leapt out and disappeared into the darkness. From that moment on, I was a man bound to the will of others. I sat huddled in my seat among my trunks and suitcases, little more than a trunk or suitcase myself. I couldn't summon the courage to ask the driver, "Have we arrived?" Eventually he turned to me and asked, "Where to now?"

"I don't know. Let's wait for my friend to return."

At last Mehmet Ali came walking back. He had a shadow in tow who couldn't have stood more than five feet tall. As he and the shadow reached in and started unloading the baggage in silence, I just as silently alighted from the carriage.

I wondered if Mehmet Ali suddenly regretted that he'd brought me to his village. Or maybe, I thought, his mother and siblings had been displeased because he'd shown up with an unexpected guest and they'd bickered while I was waiting in the carriage. Overcome by a strange feeling of sullenness, I trailed along behind my luggage. With nearly every step I stumbled into a hole in the path or tripped over a rock, slipping all the while on things that were as slick as melon rinds.

The village reeked like a mangy cow caked with the mud of a swamp.

When Mehmet Ali said, "This way, sir, step inside," I ducked through a door, which was little more than a hole in the wall, as obediently as a patient being shuffled off to a hospital ward for an operation. The floor of the room was covered in coarse straw and an old woman was standing to the side, holding a lantern.

Gesturing towards a narrow mattress in the corner, Mehmet Ali said, "Sir, please sit down." With the same obedience as before, I sat down. The woman placed the lantern on the floor and silently left. I looked up at Mehmet Ali's face as he stood in the dim light of the room, his shadow cast on the ceiling. Was he happy that I was there? Displeased? No, neither of those. Mehmet Ali was just preoccupied.

I now saw that the short man who'd helped with my luggage was a boy who looked to be maybe ten or eleven years of age. He'd stepped in and was now standing in the middle of the room, looking at me intently. After placing my baggage in a neat row along the length of the wall, Mehmet Ali left, but the boy remained rooted to the spot, still staring at me. He had more the appearance of a dwarf than a boy. Not just because he had the gaze of a grown man, but because his face was haggard, his body wiry, his movements listless.

I asked, "Are you Mehmet Ali's little brother?"

He nodded.

"So, how old are you?"

"Fourteen."

"What's your name?"

"İsmail."

"Do you go to school?"

He shrugged his shoulders, half in anger, half surprised.

"School? Who would look after things if I did? Plus, there's no school in the village. Some kids study with the imam at his place."

His eyes were still locked on mine. He looked odd in the light from the lantern on the floor, like the most malformed of scarecrows.

Hoping it would prompt him to break his gaze, I said, "Why don't you give me a hand? Let's get these bags unpacked."

It took me a long time to get settled in the room. It is a cell with a dirt floor and two small windows that look out over the plains, and from the ceiling, which consists of roughly hewn poplar logs, were hanging dried spices and plants of various sorts. My first order of business was to set up my bed and cover the ceiling with my cot's two burlap travel bags, and then lay out the wood and linoleum flooring I'd brought from the city. I set up my walnut book chest as a table and shelf for my books. My bed is the very same one I'd had in Istanbul because I've always kept my wartime travel cot. Over time, it has become part of my body, and I'm unable to sleep on anything that's more comfortable.

The biggest problem I've faced while living in the village, a most vexing issue which I've never been able to solve, is the matter of cleanliness . . . One must walk all the way to the river in order to get water, and the water there is little more than flowing sludge.

There is, of course, water in the village. However, from morning until night both the well and the public fountain are thronging with people: The elderly doing their ablutions, wives filling buckets to take home, young women splashing around, and children playing games that, suffice to say, involve unimaginable filth and mud. Sometimes women even wash their laundry there because they are too lazy to walk to the river.

For weeks on end following the harvest, grains of all kinds are rinsed in the fountain, and often food is washed together with soiled baby diapers and dirty underpants and shirts. It is simply impossible to explain to these people the unhygienic nature of what they are doing.

Mehmet Ali appears to be the only person here who acknowledges these claims of mine. He, however, is convinced that being filthy is an inherent aspect of village life, so he has no desire to bother trying to introduce any changes.

On the day we arrived, Mehmet Ali gave up everything soldierly and reverted wholly to his previous ways.

At that time, I was astonished to witness such a regression in the character of a man who had once been under my command. But when I myself started slowly undergoing a process of what I would term "villagerization," it wasn't difficult for me to attribute his transformation to the effects of the environment on people.

Training, education, and good examples are all temporary things. When the environment doesn't change, it is impossible for people to change. Starting off from this small point of deliberation, it doesn't take a stretch of the imagination to see why the drive for innovation and Westernization in Turkey has failed.

But I didn't come here just to save myself from the cruelty of the enemy. No, I came to save myself from the torment of my own mind.

Thinking—I mean thinking in this place where people live cheek and jowl with animals in earthen and stony hollows as if they were still in the Stone Age—now strikes me as shameful.

Sometimes I become tongue-tied when I am talking with the villagers about an abstract idea.

I recall one particular day. It was around noon, and we were sitting under the vine canopy of the coffeehouse. They were all there: Mehmet Ali, Bekir Çavuş, Salih Ağa, and the muhtar. The discussion was about the war and its consequences. Carefully watching their expressions, I was telling them about how Istanbul had been occupied by the armies of four countries, how the Greeks were pushing forward from Izmir up through Bursa, how the French still had not withdrawn from Adana, and how bloody atrocities were taking place in Urfa and Antep. None of them expressed an ounce of shock or horror. Not even the blandest response. As for Mehmet Ali, who had just returned from the war, he was listening as if I was relating a tale that belonged to the distant past.

"Mehmet Ali knows about it. In Istanbul, the sultan, the state, and the government weren't left with a shred of dignity. Mere captains from those armies give the grand vizier orders. They advise the sultan, telling him to appoint so-and-so to a certain position or relieve so-and-so of their duties. If he doesn't do as they said, they come pounding on the palace door, swinging their whips. As for the common people, every possible torment has been inflicted on them. High-ranking officials and our great thinkers were shipped off to Malta, and no one could say a word about it. Everyone has to pay fines for the most preposterous things. They say to one person, 'You were holding that chicken upside down, so pay up. Five lira.' They say to someone else, 'You were talking too loudly on the tram. That's ten lira.'"

I looked around at their faces. They didn't seem to find anything I was saying to be odd in the least. Switching tactics, I tried to strike an emotional chord with them. I said, "After they were finished raping and plundering, nothing was left. The honor of our women was in tatters, our children had been slaughtered, our religion and faith were razed. They took it all." I went on expounding on such matters. Then I noticed that the muhtar was snoozing, Mehmet Ali was whittling a willow stick, and Salih Ağa was watching a flock of sheep grazing on a hillside. Only Bekir Çavuş showed the slightest interest in what I had to say.

"Sir," he asked, "do you think there'll be another war?"

"It's already started," I replied. "Haven't you heard? A great man by the name of Mustafa Kemal, a great commander, travelled from

Istanbul to Anatolia. He's rallying the people in Erzurum and Sivas, telling them that the government isn't functioning and that we need to drive off the enemy and protect ourselves. Now he and his men are fighting the Greeks and the French. They're all great heroes . . ."

I tried to rouse their feelings with glorious accounts of the army's feats. Because Mehmet Ali had been on the front lines in the Battle of Gallipoli, he knew of Mustafa Kemal, so I glanced at him. Examining the stick of willow for a moment, he turned to me.

"Sir, I can only hope," he said, "that they won't make us join the army again."

That was the saddest day for me since I'd arrived in the village.

*

While Salih Ağa is one of the wealthier residents of the village, in terms of appearance, he is no different than a panhandler. I can't ever remember him wearing socks, even on the coldest winter days. Those darkened feet of his with cracked heels which had squashed down the back of his shoes revealed far more than his hands. It wouldn't be an exaggeration to say that the sum total of his guileful personality and very self had converged in his feet. Was he feeling at ease? Was he irritated? Was he about to swindle a villager in a dispute about a piece of land? Did he just make a handsome profit? Did he suffer a loss? What does he think about you? Look at his feet if you want to understand such matters.

If Salih Ağa is rubbing one of his toes, it means something is bothering him. If he's lightly brushing one of his shoes with his toes, you know he's in high spirits. If he's sitting still, pointing a bare sole in the direction of your face, you can be certain that he's in the process of digesting the spoils of something he's recently seized. But if he's plotting against you, his feet will be tucked under him, hidden from sight.

If you've never seen how a fox slyly trots while approaching its prey, all you need to do is watch how Salih Ağa walks to understand what it looks like.

Salih Ağa held everyone in the village under his sway and spell, so much so that even Mehmet Ali, who had been under my command for four years, told me as soon as we arrived in the village that I should speak to the man so I could consult him about how to build on my finances.

"Sir, he's a very smart man. He'll tell you just what you need to do."

But instead of turning to him, I prefer to do absolutely nothing and make do with what I have.

When I sold the house in Istanbul that I'd inherited from my father, my plan had been to use the money to buy a small house surrounded by gardens in an Anatolian village. The gardens were going to ensure I had an income, and I was going to live out the rest of my life in that little home. In this village, however, the land simply wouldn't do. While the Porsuk River does run near the village, it would take a major canalization project to make the planting of gardens feasible, a pricey and laborious task as immense as the reed beds and swamps on this side of the river. And in any case, there isn't a soul in the village who knows anything about planting such crops.

But in Western Anatolia, I saw the greenest, most beautiful set of gardens. In the center was a well around which plodded a beast of burden wearing blinders as it spun a large cogwheel that drove a system for drawing out the water. At times the cogwheel sounded like a woman weeping and at others it was reminiscent of a child's laughter. One after the other steel buckets rose from the well, dumping out their contents, only to plunge back into its depths. It was summer at the time of my visit, early evening, and the buzz of the cicadas in the poplar trees hadn't yet fallen silent for the year. Long, narrow, straight channels carried the glistening water off to fields of lettuce.

Among the broad rectangular pattern of channels that had been cut into the soil, there was a man with a small hoe who looked like he was performing prayers for a sect that worshipped nature as he slowly bowed, rose up, bowed, and crouched down over and over again as he worked the ground. And you, lazing under a trellis, are the spectator of this spectacle.

The air smells of moist earth.

In recent times, that has been my one and only dream.

*

But here, there is only reality; bare, repulsive, crude, craggy reality! Waves of grizzled earth stretching as far as the eye can see. The Porsuk River, which cuts the drab plains in two, is like a long, serpentine cleft in the ground ripped open by a violent earthquake. Its waters go unseen. Even when you approach it, you find nothing of life-giving coolness or color. The ashen earth rots on its banks and congeals. If you dip your hand into the river, regardless of the time of day or season, it is as warm as pus.

And the hills . . . The hills are as tumors. And the world encircled by the horizon only seems to come alive with that panorama of anguish.

In all the emptiness and inanity of the firmament above, not once have I seen a bird flit past.

God should not have gone to the trouble of creating the punishment of the Great Flood to test humanity's faith. He should have just cast Noah's people onto these lands encircled by barren hills.

Every evening I think that the end of the world is drawing near.

Heaving with secret sorrows, this ground upon which we live will either swell and burst open or it will collapse, caving in on itself with a terrific roar.

That's why, as soon as I open my eyes every morning, I am met with a heavy disappointment. "Why," I ask myself, "has the calamity I expected not befallen us?" And the creatures creeping down from the flat rooftops share in my astonishment.

So, one more day? And what a day!

With every step he takes as he drives his herd of sheep in front of him, Emeti's orphan boy lashes their backs, coughing and hacking like an old man. As they roll their large encrusted eyes in their sockets, the black water buffalo, which are more wrinkled and ill-tempered than elephants, scrounge around for something to eat. In the village's rubbish heap, pups and little children tumble around together in play—until one of the children comes upon a scrap of food, whereupon a puppy lunges in for the attack, and then the child in turn snatches at the morsel between its paws. You might even see a water buffalo muzzle in and devour the rind of a melon that a puppy and child are scuffling over.

Out of hunger and ennui, the donkeys that aren't taken out to work bray plaintively from dawn till dusk. Ah, that braying of the donkeys! Could there be a more mournful, a more dolorous sound in the world? Even when they fall silent, their manner is no less sorrowful than their cries. There is woe in their deep, dark, velvety eyes, quivering emotion in their beautiful long ears, and the charming solemnity of sagacious judges in their minds.

I truly love these animals. In the midst of all this crude, vulgar nature, they are the only sweet, amiable creatures.

Mehmet Ali's family has a grey donkey which looks after all of the housework, doing the labor of what they call in the large cities a "bonne a tout faire," or a housemaid. Except that it doesn't cook. Or wash laundry, or do ironing. In any case, two of those are but rarely done here, and one of them, never.

That is the donkey which carries not only Mehmet Ali but also his mother and brother to town a few times a month.

The good things that Mehmet Ali's mother makes at home are never eaten or drunk, not even tasted, by anyone. She takes them to the market to sell. Then again, I've obtained a certain amount of those things. By paying double what they would cost in town, I'm able to get some oil, yogurt, cheese, and sausage. But even in such cases, she doesn't seem happy with the situation and mumbles to herself because in her mind, true riches are made in the market. That's why, without telling anyone, she usually slips off early in the morning when she goes to town. And it's a long trip. If you ask the villagers, they'll tell you, "Weeell, town's just right over there," but I know what that means. The shortest "Well . . ." takes five or six hours.

I wondered why they don't make a connection between the concepts of distance and time.

But as the days went by, I found the answer to that question myself. Since I've been here, I've been losing grasp of the passage of time. In the first few months, I started losing track of the days. Now, I get the months confused. All I notice is that the seasons are changing.

God knows what a relief I'll feel when I forget my own age and the past I've left behind! But even then, the horrific vastness of these broad, arid plains will haunt me. Every waking moment I'm tormented by how it grips my heart, makes me dizzy, and cracks my will.

Squatting in the middle of a desert landscape, this village doesn't offer a league of reassurance, much less a mile. A league, as in how far a person walks in an hour, represents movement across a distance. Now you're here, and in an hour you'll reach an oasis. In a few more hours, you'll be met by the shores of a sweeping river. But a village in central Anatolia is a frozen league. Here, distance swallows you up. Within the span of distance, you are frozen in fear.

Truly, how are the people in this village, which is like the ruins of a far-flung Hittite settlement, any different from chipped, broken statues freshly pried from the ground?

Sometimes Bekir Çavuş and I talk about the places he's seen during his travels, the extent of which he is boastful about. In his mind, the reason why the people in the village are so backwards is that they have not travelled the land.

"Ah, sir, just think about it. We're talking about twenty-three years in the military here. I've seen it all: Rumelia, Damascus, Crete . . ."

And one by one he names the places he's seen. For him, the world is like a long strip that started here in this village and ended here as well. And the cities, countries, continents, and islands, one after the other, are points representing distances travelled.

"In Crete," he says, "I saw them making soap. There they don't pound the olives in mortars like they do here. They've got machines. You put olives in one end and olive oil comes out the other. The seeds go to one place, the stems to another, and what's left of the olives to another. Freshest oil you can get. Fresh as the water in Istanbul. As for the soap . . ."

"Damascus? Oh God, after seeing that place, I wouldn't pay a cent for a place in the other world. All those trees, all that water . . . Just like how the imam here describes heaven. Believe me when I tell you I saw eight different kinds of fruit there. I counted them. And the watermelons! Sweet as honey, like the ones from Aleppo. Then there's the watermelons from Tulkarem. Not even five people could pick one up."

Bekir Çavuş's tales about other countries never fail to gently stir my imagination. Every word, every story, every image sweeps me away from this place, filling me with an excitement that is virtually aesthetic.

One day when Bekir Çavuş was telling me about the water or fruit from some place, I asked him:

"What about the women?"

That fifty-year-old man suddenly looked down as abashed as a child, a broad grin on his face.

I'd been in the village for maybe seven or eight months when the incident occurred. I say "incident" because the question which so spontaneously fell from my lips was proof that I'd reached an emotional state worthy of note.

The heat that sears my skin in these barren lands is slowly enveloping my insides as well, scorching my heart. Water, shade, greenery . . . That's not all I lack. Since the day I arrived here, I haven't seen a single creature I'd call a woman, or even a girl. All the same, there has been a wedding since I've been here, the wedding of Mehmet Ali no less. And I was there.

Two months after our arrival, Mehmet Ali took a girl from a neighboring village to be his bride. And although it was the third time he was getting married, he was regaled like a first-time groom.

But what a dreary, morose and vulgar wedding it was! Without a doubt, the funerals in Europe are cheerier affairs. During the ceremony, which lasted three days and three nights, the most miserable person I saw was Mehmet Ali himself, as he was suddenly thrust into a state of uselessness, condemned to sitting in a corner and watching people come and go, eat and drink, and dance in their finest attire. The strange thing was that the bride was nowhere to be seen.

In the mornings, the elders and notables of the village would sit at the foot of a wall, and I would join them. Most of the wedding attendees were teenage boys and girls, but there were also some men over forty. And suddenly the crowd was transformed into a small cluster of people, mostly women and a few men. Linking arms, they danced in opposing circles. The dances were slow and monotonous, consisting of movements to the right and left punctuated with hops.

The shrill notes of a cracked *zurna* and the thumping of a *darbuka* that seemed to be a cross between a drum and a gourd splintered the air.

As I sat at the foot of the wall, I tried to smile and appear interested. Once in a while I tossed a lira in the direction of a man who was imitating the old epic dances, clutching a stick instead of a spear and a plank of wood in place of a shield. With every coin I tossed, my prestige rose . . . And a new wave of enthusiasm seemed to fill the dancers.

The women of the village were there before me, all of them wearing new dresses for the occasion, and their rows of gold bracelets jangled like bells when they raised their arms in dance. But most of the women were unshapely, squat, chubby, or big-boned, and while some of them, despite the layers of fabric in which they were ensconced, aroused the feeling that they had elegant, fresh, bosomy bodies, as soon as you looked at their hands or feet, that alluring impression fell away.

It was the visits that tormented me the most about the wedding. When the neighbors showed up bringing copper platters heaping with various kinds of food, I didn't know what I was supposed to do. A woman was going around, holding up her outer skirt which was filled with bread, or rather, thin sheets of rolled-out dough, a fistful of which she dropped in front of each guest, and then all at the same time hands dove into the platters. I saw Mehmet Ali's hands among them, distinguishable by the henna on his palms.

I sighed to myself, "I've no choice but to accustom myself to all this." But Mehmet Ali's wedding ceremony seemed to dash all my efforts at assimilation.

At long last, the bride was brought out of the house and thrust into the throng, as lifeless and nondescript as a bundle of clothes tied up in a cloth.

How do birds make love? How do cats make love? Those things I know. But I have no idea how the people in this village make love. As we do, looking into each other's eyes? Grasping hands? Do their lips come together in a kiss? How do they caress one another? When their hearts swell and spill over like simmering pots of milk, what is the meaning of the sounds they make, what is the harmony?

After Mehmet Ali got married, those questions became a matter of deliberation for me.

The women of Anatolia are so lacking in coquetry, coyness, and the art of playful wiles that if I were to lie bosom to bosom with one of them, my arm wrapped around her, my body would likely not respond in the least. And I surmise that they smell anything but pleasant.

Maybe it's because they instinctively sense how I feel about them—I can't quite be sure—but whenever we cross paths, those women turn their backs to me, or they crouch down, pulling their headscarves further up over their heads, like grieving women would do in ancient Greece. I quickly noticed that they don't behave like that with any of the other men in the village.

After I'd been in the village a number of weeks, I asked Mehmet Ali, "Why do the women here avoid me so?"

"Sir, because you're an outsider. That's why."

At first, I was filled with indignation at being called an "outsider." Later, however, I came to understand that people from the villages of Anatolia call anyone they don't know an "outsider," not unlike how the Greeks of the past referred to others as "barbarians."

One day . . . One day, I wonder, will I be able to prove to them that I am not an "outsider"? The blood in my veins is the same blood that flows through their veins. The language I speak is the language they speak. Our ancestors trod the same historical and geographical path that brought us here. Will I be able to prove that we were created by the same God? We are bound together by the same political fate, the same social ties, which transcend even familial bonds.

But how shall I convey such notions? I already find it difficult to express myself clearly enough to obtain the most trivial of my daily needs, so how could I expect to speak with them about such matters?

Day by day, the situation becomes clearer to me: The Turkish "intellectual," the Turkish luminary, is a strange, lonely figure in the vast, desolate world of this land known as Turkey.

Is he a recluse? No, I'd do better to call him an odd creature. Envisage someone whose species or race are not apparent. As he probes the depths of the country he takes to be his homeland, he feels himself growing ever distant from his roots. Even if he doesn't feel it, the emptiness that opens up around him, the cold driving air, constantly makes it clear to him that he is an incongruity, a bizarre plant that has been plucked from its soil.

In other countries, is there also a gaping chasm between rural society and the educated class? I don't know. But there is a greater difference between someone educated in Istanbul and a villager from Anatolia than an English Londoner and an Indian from Punjab.

As I write this, my hand trembles.

Since the day I arrived here, the most pressing issue for me has been, starting with Mehmet Ali's family, getting the people here accustomed to me, getting them to warm up to my presence. Until now, however—and I've been here for eight months—I don't think I've succeeded, perhaps with the exception of little İsmail and Mehmet Ali's mother Zeynep *Kadın*.

Granted, I'm on good terms with most of the men here. We have friendly conversations under the trees, by the public fountain, on the banks of the river, and at the coffeehouse. But it's such a shallow, tenuous friendship that I can tell they're not satisfied with it, and neither am I. In their dealings with me, their hearts and minds seem to be tightly bound in swathes of cloth, and our conversations always revolve around complaints about the soil, the weather, or time.

In all truth, Mehmet Ali's mother and I talk about nothing else. I sense, however, that lurking beneath the surface of this gruff, severe, yet resigned woman who, as a widow of twelve years, has been the sole provider for her family, there lies a strength steeped in the vigor of nature. Is she forty years old? In her fifties perhaps? It's impossible to tell. Her hands and feet are like tree roots fixed firmly in the depths of the earth, and I know that her body is as hardy as the trunk of an oak.

Time and time again I've seen her carry off loads—without even breaking a sweat—that were too heavy for their small donkey to bear, and she labors for hours bent over in the fields, not once stopping to straighten her back. One day she got into an argument with a neighbor over who had the right to use a certain millstone, and, unwilling to back down, she shoved the massive stone onto its side.

Although she's usually quite calm, you never know what Zeynep Kadın will do when she flies into a fit of rage. Once İsmail was late coming home from town. She started laying into him with such violence that I couldn't pull him from her grasp, not even with Mehmet Ali's help.

It was during that incident that I saw Mehmet's wife and sisters. As soon as they spotted me, they scampered off like frightened chickens in a coop.

İsmail wasn't crying. His demeanor was calm and grave, as if he'd just been carrying out a laborious task. Only when I managed to wrest him free of his mother's grip and drag him off to my room did I hear his heart pounding in his sunken chest like the wild thudding of an iron knocker, seemingly loud enough to crack his breastbone. How then, I wondered, was he able to escape unscathed?

I always ask myself that about the weak, frail, and infirm. What hidden power protects these people who are constantly being battered by the forces of nature which are a hundred times more brutal than Zeynep Kadın, driving them to go on with their lives?

That's a question for you, o womb of Zeynep Kadın!

After that ferocious thrashing, İsmail sat cowering in a corner of my room, and after a while he fell asleep.

I looked at his small, quivering body, which was little more than a lump of flesh that had been beaten down on all sides. His head had disappeared between his arms and knees. If I hadn't heard the sound of his breathing in the silence of my room, I might have mistaken him for a heap of rags.

That poor creature knows nothing of childhood. While children in distant places revel in the joy of youth, knowing nothing but laughter and play, İsmail is burdened with grueling labor that would test the strength of a twenty-year old man. He carries loads. He hoes the fields. And all the while consumption tears at his chest with its venomous claws. I wonder if he's ever laughed.

I doubt it. I've seen the small children here, three or four years old. They all look like they're wearing masks of forty-year-old men's faces. Even their gait is that of weary, grown men. When seen from behind, you get the impression that they are downtrodden, glum dwarves.

Hadn't I thought that about İsmail when I first arrived here? Over time I grew accustomed to thinking of him as a child and started to love him as such. As I watched him that night, a feeling of pity stirred deep within me, pooling in my heart as tears. I walked over to him and stroked his back.

Luckless village boy! You are the child of two step-mothers. One is the woman who beats you, and the other is your homeland which has been bludgeoning you day after day since you were born. And you trudge through life, suffering the pain of both.

Soon enough you will become a young man. But when that happens . . .

Yet again I can see in my mind's eye the men from the war, how they were barefoot when they showed up to enlist, their shirts and baggy trousers in tatters, and then how they died, toppling backwards onto the ground or falling on their faces, clad in khaki.

And I can hear the voice of a soldier murmuring to himself in the trenches: "What should I be scared of? Every day they shoot at us but they always miss."

As he spoke those words, of course there was an enemy airplane snarling overhead.

I still haven't cut myself off from the world in the way I'd wanted. Every once in a while I get copies of the Istanbul newspapers, and that's how I found out about the battle of İnönü where we won our first victory. For days I was ecstatic.

In the village I was telling everyone who crossed my path about it. I spoke of nothing else, and no one escaped my clutches, not the women who turned their backs to me on the street nor the children who fled in fear when they saw me coming. Mehmet Ali's mother, sister, wife, and little brother, and especially Mehmet Ali himself, were on the brink of exasperation.

The villagers, who already had little faith in the soundness of my mental faculties, must have thought I'd completely lost my mind.

Then the moment came when I started doubting myself as well, so I reined in my joy, placing it within certain bounds.

Curbing one's anguish, sorrow, even delight . . . I'd always thought people only did that in the cities. But as I realized, we cannot be genuine anywhere, not in villages, out in the wild, or in the depths of caves, nor are we possessed of the freedom to weep or laugh as our feelings spring forth within us. The traditions and injunctions of society prevail with the same severity in these mole burrows inhabited by half-naked wretches.

And what could be stranger than seeing a happy man in these wasted lands? Since the day the earthen walls of this village were raised, I'm sure they have never echoed with laughter. A solemn, resigned air reigns supreme, never to ripple with the sounds of festive tumult.

I think back on the night when Mehmet Ali and I first arrived. The shadow of the mother, who set the lamp on the floor and silently stepped out. The tragic, pinched face of a gaunt boy.

Then there was Mehmet Ali's wedding. That day was drearier than all the rest. The cracked zurna, the listless dancing, the bland food.

But after the victory of İnönü, I am untroubled by such matters.

Still, I wonder: Where is the rejoicing? Where the jubilation? Was this momentous occasion brushed aside in the papers as humdrum news? In some city, some town, were the telegrams between Mustafa Kemal and İsmet Pasha not emblazoned in the sky in flames, line by line, for all to see?

When the newspapers arrive, I pore over them, searching for a hint of triumph. But in vain. Maybe in some remote Anatolian village, Ankara perhaps, a few lamps have been strung up here and there, the only glad radiance commemorating that victory. In my imagination, I light such lamps myself, and they appear to me as the sole spark of life in the cold, blind hearts of the people inhabiting this dark realm of exile.

But what a dull, lackluster spark of life! One day will these people be able to set the gray plains of Anatolia ablaze with the glow of grandeur? If only I knew that would happen . . . If only I knew.

After spending a few days in town, the muhtar returned to the village with a smattering of news and new ideas. Although he shares little with me, I've learned to glean the unspoken from what he says. And by completing his unfinished sentences with what I've heard from others, I can pin down what's on his mind.

In his opinion, the path on which Mustafa Kemal has set out is a dead end. It is a dead end because the Sultan is not backing him and because the Sultan already made peace with the enemy. Then there is the issue of that queen known as "Europe" who complicated matters but then said, "I'll handle your hardships for you."

It's a dangerous path because while the enemy is building up its forces in Izmir, Mustafa Kemal, enraged by their actions, is driving his army towards them and has already reached Bursa, where he pushed on to the town of İnönü.

Trembling with anger, I say, "We drove them out. Not just that, we routed them."

The muhtar smirks behind his white beard. I want to shake him by the shoulders and shout, "What are you smiling about?"

Sensing my anger, the villagers start drifting away one by one, and the muhtar shuffles off with them, scratching the back of his neck. Once they are a certain distance away, they stop and huddle together in hushed conversation.

Seeing that I'm alone, Mehmet Ali timidly approaches. He squats down beside me and starts poking at the dirt with the willow branch he was carving the other day, unsure of how he should start. Then he blurts, "Sir, are they going to make us join the army again?"

"Maybe."

"What do you mean, 'maybe'? Weren't we discharged?"

"Yes, but the enemy doesn't care about such things. They're already marching on us now. If we listen carefully, we can almost hear the sound of their cannons. If they come charging over that hill, are you going to just stand by? As they burn down the village and beat your family with the butts of their rifles, are you going to run off and hide like a woman?"

"No sir, but I really don't think they'll make it this far."

"If the people in other villages act like the people here, and if our soldiers are afraid to go back into battle like you, then of course they'll come. You can be certain of that."

Mehmet Ali starts scratching at the dirt again with his stick.

He's a complete stranger to me now. There's nothing left of the private I once knew. I get the urge to snap, "Go on, go be with the others," and pack my things so I can leave the village as quickly as possible.

Would I be completely useless on the front lines? In the end, what does it matter? My missing arm is nothing but an excuse concocted for myself and the world at large.

Little by little my anger at the villagers is metamorphosing into self-loathing. Getting up, I start walking down toward the plains.

It is April. Banks of clouds are piling up on the horizon and I can smell rain in the air, although the ground beneath my feet is dry, hard, and scentless.

The past winter brought bitter freezes. The villagers watched, stricken with fear, as scores of their livestock died. Salih Ağa has said there will be a meager harvest this year.

I walk and walk, wishing that I could go on walking for hours, days, months, never stopping, but I know that these barren undulating hills are endless. When you crest the top of one, another appears before you. I'm going to leave that village behind. In a few hours, one just like it will appear in the distance. And again I will flee. Yet again I will flee.

How far can the Porsuk River take me? When I come upon it, I start walking along its banks. Once in a while I trip over a willow root jutting up from the earth. Such listless, indolent, miserable trees those willows. A stench rises up from the muck of the riverside.

It is midday. Occasionally the sun breaks through the clouds, burning the nape of my neck. Spring is so fine in other parts of the country. Of course, when I say that I mean the outskirts of Istanbul. Feneryolu, Göztepe, Erenköy . . .

My heart quivers in my chest like a mischievous child locked in a dank room with no windows. I think of leaving my money with Salih Ağa and my books and belongings at Mehmet Ali's place and walking, walking, all the way to Istanbul.

While I know it's an impossible dream, I keep going as though Istanbul really is at the end of my path. My eyes nearly closed, I walk on, oblivious to the mountains, rivers, and treacherous passes that lie ahead and the fact that I would have to make it past the towns of Sakarya, Bozdağ, and Acıdağ, casting from my thoughts a singular truth: Even if I wanted, I couldn't cross the swift, murky river in front of me.

Distracted by daydreams, I don't know how far I've walked, but I find myself in a copse of poplars and I stop.

A small, clear stream flows among the trees, and the air is cool. I wonder if I've stumbled upon an oasis. A profound feeling of tranquility washes over me. As I kneel down, dipping my hand into the water, I hear a rustling. And what's that? A woman's muffled giggle?

I look around. Off to the left I see the silhouette of a young woman as she darts into the shadows of the trees as lithely as a deer.

She stops and turns to look at me.

I'm astounded that such a place exists just a few hours from the village. And such a lovely face! It's inconceivable.

As she smiles at me across the distance between us, I see a row of large white teeth, green eyes, and the dark olive skin of her oval face. She's dressed like the women from Mehmet Ali's village. Her head is wrapped in windings of cloth, a sash is tied around her waist, and she's wearing a thick cotton dress. Why has such a marvel appeared before my eyes?

I smile back at her as she lingers half-hidden behind a tree.

Should I approach her? Perhaps she would take fright and flee. I kneel down towards the water again, but I can feel her gaze on me with every ounce of my being. Quickly I look up and she slips back behind the tree. This, I think, is some kind of game.

I murmur to myself, "Is she human or djinn? If she's djinn, she should've vanished by now. If she's human, why's she hiding?"

Out of the corner of my eye, I peer at her. She's standing perfectly still. My patience wearing thin, I call out to her: "Don't be afraid. Go on with what you were doing. I'm no stranger." I tell her the name of the village where I'm staying and ask, "Which village are you from?"

In a faint voice, she says from behind the tree, "My village is close by. Just right over there . . ."

She tells me the name of her village.

That brief conversation, however, doesn't bridge the distance between us. After taking another drink from the stream, I get to my feet and take a few steps towards her.

"I'll leave you be," I say. "I'm going." And I jump across the stream.

On the stream's other bank, I'm now a completely different man.

*

My mind is still in disarray after that encounter. When I leapt over the stream, I felt like a weight was lifted from me. As if a cannonball

I'd been carrying around in my heart, in my mind, had suddenly fallen free. Now I feel light. So light that if I were to flap my arm like a wing, I'd take to the skies.

The heart is such a strange thing. One day, in the middle of a copse of poplars: A young woman's smile, a stream, a leap. And then everything changed. There isn't a trace left of the man who existed before that moment.

What happened to him? Did he melt away? Who is this man who took his place? What is he?

If I were to tell myself that I've fallen in love, it would be sheer folly. I'm well into my thirties now, the detritus of a man who suffered misadventures in life. Even ten years ago I wasn't naïve in matters of love. When it comes to women, this warm, gentle, spirited heart of mine is well-versed in the art of being cold and distant. It is sweeter to beguile the fairer sex than hang on the words that fall from their lips because there is nothing more insufferable than a woman who feels she's loved. At one point or another, her fickle, craven nature gives rise to traits that border on lethal. Surpassing the wildness of the feline and venomousness of the serpentine, she swims nude in the sea of iniquity, which is deeper, vaster, and brinier than we could ever imagine.

I did not arrive at that truth through bitter personal experience. In my life, love always came about as the result of the exigencies of sexuality. In that sense, I was no different than animals suffering from crises brought on by the fervor of the mating season.

*

For two days now an air of exceptional times has been hanging over the village. Is it a holiday? Apparently not, because people aren't strutting around in their finest outfits. Is someone getting married? It's not that either. But all the same, I've noticed that, instead of working, the villagers have been holding gatherings at each other's homes which I'd venture to say are rather secretive. And there's a general sense of giddiness and a glimmer in people's eyes to which I'm rather unaccustomed. I've even caught Mehmet Ali's mother smiling, which makes her look twenty years younger.

Bekir Çavuş has been going around, whispering in people's ears: "He's here . . ."

"He's here. At Ahmet's place now."

"He's here. Haven't you seen him?"

"He's here. But I don't think he'll stay long."

I pulled Mehmet Ali aside.

"What's going on?"

He too seemed captivated by the overall atmosphere of excitement. Grinning, he said, "Nothing, sir."

But when I pressed him further, he opened up. "Sir, Dervish Yusuf is here."

"And who is this Dervish Yusuf?"

"A holy man. A great man. He comes every year and we ask him to pray for us. He recites prayers for people who are sick and makes them better, and he gives us advice about what we should do. And he helps those who are going through hard times."

"Which order is he from?"

"That much I don't know, sir."

"What has he done to help out the people here?"

"Lots, sir," he replied, nodding mysteriously. "The only person he hasn't healed is the muhtar's wife."

"What about Salih Ağa's hunchbacked son? Has he helped him?"

" . . . "

"Or Bekir Çavuş's daughter. Has he cured her blindness?"

" . . . "

"Has he cured Memiş of his lunacy?"

Mehmet Ali looked down in silence. I could tell he was getting angry. But I went on, blither and more contemptuous than before:

"And this advice he gives. Tell me about that."

"I can't remember now, sir. My mother would know."

Hoping to slip free of my questioning, he called her over. The old woman said, "What would Mehmet Ali know about things like that? Efendi Dervish Yusuf is a pillar of wisdom."

"Then tell me about what he says."

"How would I even begin?"

The only recourse was to implore Dervish Yusuf to come to our place.

Mehmet Ali took on that troublesome task and rushed off to the muhtar's house, but he returned as quickly as he'd left. The muhtar had told him, "Why would he do such a thing? You're the one who should be going to see him." Since we had no other choice, we set off. The room at the muhtar's house in which Dervish Yusuf was seated was crowded from wall to wall with people from the village. He was sitting cross-legged on a straw mat in the corner wearing a robe that had probably once been green. So filthy were his raiment and beard that the stench—which was like the odor of a randy billy goat—filled the room.

When the small crowd of people caught sight of me stepping into the room with Mehmet Ali and his mother in tow, they started to disperse.

Sitting down, I said, "Peace be upon you, Dervish Yusuf."

He looked up with the annoyance of a man disturbed from a reverie and, after scowling at me for a while, he grunted toothlessly, "And just who are you to wish peace on me?"

The muhtar cut in, "Forgive us. He's a stranger here."

With great difficulty I resisted the urge to strike both the dervish and the muhtar in the face with one balled up fist. Forcing a smile through gritted teeth, I replied, "You're not only in need of peace, but manners as well."

As soon as those words left my mouth, that old billy goat leapt to his feet with astounding agility. After grabbing his sandals, which were by the door, and tucking them under his arm, he stormed outside.

Everyone ran after him, even Mehmet Ali.

Feeling a little startled and sheepish, I slowly got to my feet. Much later I laughed until my sides ached as I thought back on how that meeting unfolded, especially towards the end, but that day my misery knew no bounds. Never before had I felt like such an outsider, shunned and completely alone, and those emotions weighed on me with singular intensity.

I saw no difference between that dotard of a Turkish dervish and the English officers stationed in Istanbul, as the chasm between their psyches and mine was equally deep and dark. Both would take pleasure in flogging me or locking me in a dungeon until I rotted away.

If I were in the home of a fanatical Protestant priest in London, would I not be treated with the same haughty disdain? Would I not feel the same sorrow, the same grief of the forsaken outcast, that haunts me now?

*

Because of me, Dervish Yusuf cut short his visit this year. I saw him as he was leaving. Both he and his donkey were staggering down the path, bowed down under the weight of the villagers' gifts.

Dervish Yusuf was gone. But his poison lingered in the village. For a while, a very long while, the air was filled with his breath.

The villagers no longer feel a need to be angry with or despise me. Their only emotion is pity. In me they see a man condemned, a cursed man sentenced to fall under the executioner's blade.

I can see the question in their eyes: What will become of this poor creature who has incurred the wrath of the dervish?

And I flee those barbed glances, seeking refuge in the oasis I discovered the other day. Only there can I truly be myself and find respite from my thoughts.

It is cool among the poplars and the stream runs clear. But I haven't seen a trace of that faerie of the grove. I ask myself, "Perhaps the woman you saw that day was nothing but a figment of your imagination?" I try to conjure her up in my mind's eye.

One day I walked all the way to her village. I strolled the streets and chatted with a few of the villagers, and although I saw some women coming back from washing their laundry, she wasn't among them. But then at last . . .

As I was walking yet again from the grove to her village, who should I come across?

Together with a rather homely young woman, she was carrying a long wooden tub filled with shirts, şalvar, and scarves. She was holding up the front of the tub as they made their way down the path. When she saw me, she used her free hand to pull her headscarf across her face and looked the other direction. But I sensed that her white teeth were gleaming beneath her scarf.

I took a few more steps towards the village and then turned around. As I did so, I recalled the days of ambling along behind women along the promenades of Istanbul, and I felt like I was back on the waterfront of Kuşdili Meadow and Yoğurtçu Creek.

What's the difference between this village girl and the other girls from her neighborhood? Is her figure not slender and her gait not graceful, and is she not enticing? I'm certain that she goes around barefoot and that her heels are cracked. But I can feel the allure of her inviting, youthful body which is wrapped in those folds of rough cloth.

At one point she glanced over her shoulder, and my heart started pounding. She probably said something to her friend (or maybe it was her sister), because she too looked back in my direction and the two of them burst out laughing. As I was about to come abreast of them, they stopped in their tracks and turned around, glowering at me.

I had never seen such behavior in the female species. When a young man displays ardent desire for a woman, her body may melt under his gaze or, conversely, tense up with a violent passion that invites a carnal struggle. But what I saw that day broke with everything I knew. She was a steel tower, the epitome of stubborn defiance.

Virginity here is like a suit of armor.

*

So why was Süleyman's poor wife an exception? Let me explain.

There's a man here by the name of Süleyman. Not long after Mehmet Ali got married, he too got a girl from a nearby village but it turned out she'd been defiled before they got married. Süleyman asked, "Who did this to you?" She replied, "When I was little, we were playing in the fields. The landowner grabbed me by the shoulders. He pushed me down to the ground, squeezing me. Whatever it was, that's when it happened."

"Just say it was an accident," Süleyman said. But can villagers hold their tongues? There was no end to the backbiting. But after a while, they backed down.

Not six months later, however, Cennet—that's the woman's name—was caught one night by the wall of a sheep pen with another man. Grabbing sticks, hoes, and goads, everyone in the village charged in to attack the open-air fornicators, who took shelter behind the wall and hurled so many stones at their assailants that they were forced to beat a hasty retreat. Like a young woman taken captive in the age of Homer, Cennet clambered atop the wall and shouted, "The only person I'll turn myself over to is my husband!"

Süleyman went and, taking her by the hand, led her home. She said there was no cause for gossip because the man was her cousin and they'd run into each other by the pen, where they sat down to talk . . .

After her victory, the villagers left Cennet alone because she'd come to be seen as an exemplar of strength and determination.

Cennet is a courageous, attractive, hawk-eyed woman who is quick to laugh. She darkens her eyebrows with kohl and dyes her hands with henna. Unlike the other women in the village, she doesn't shy away from men, and even when I'm around she goes about her business, head held high. Whether she's hoeing in the fields, cooking at home, or washing laundry in the river, there's always a song on her lips.

Süleyman, on the other hand, is in many ways like a simpering child. They say that Cennet cuffs him on the ear on occasion. He is, in every sense, like Keloğlan from the Turkish folk tales of yore. Obedient, hen-pecked, and a bit of a philosopher, he has a soul of infinite depth. Sometimes he is like Âşık Garip, at other times Yunus Emre. Nasreddin Hodja is of the same lineage. The story of the Phoenix was created for the likes of him, and he's also reminiscent of the hero in "The Shepherd and the Daughter of the Fairy King," who learned the art of patience on endless journeys and acquired simplicity of character by keeping company with birds and wolves, by which means he adopted a lofty principle of living.

Ever since I found out about Süleyman's trials and tribulations, I've been one of his closest companions, though we've never sat down to share our woes.

In the eyes of others, Süleyman is a strange fellow. The most recent incidents in his life left him withdrawn yet savage, but he gets along well with young children and Mad Memiş is one of his best friends. Sometimes they sit for hours together in the ruins of the old mosque.

Süleyman says but one word in the span of thirty minutes or so, and in lieu of a reply, Memiş smiles or nods his head.

They light cigarettes and, depending on the wind, the smoke either hangs over their heads in thick, heavy rings or spirals upward like smoke from a censer.

On many occasions Cennet has caught her husband idling away the time in such a manner. Stepping atop a stone block, she bellows, hands on her hips, "You good-for-nothing! Just look at you!" whereupon Süleyman leaps to his feet and, shuffling towards her, he slowly mumbles in a weak, trembling voice, "I'm coming, I'm coming . . ."

"I thought you were going to town today!"

"Tomorrow I'll go, God willing. I couldn't today."

"What do you mean you 'couldn't'? What kept you from going?"

"I had to bring up some water. And I fixed the corner of the roof that collapsed."

"You call that work?"

"Someone knocked down the log that we use to cross the stream. Probably some kids. Anyways, I put it back."

They have such conversations on their way home, but as soon as Cennet steps through the door, she heads back out again, usually stopping at the public fountain. Often she wears earrings, and the rows of gold coins she wears on a chain around her neck glint in the sunlight. She leaves the top buttons of her blouse undone, and as her tongue wags in conversation with the other women, her eyes are just as busy eyeing the men passing by.

Is she not unlike the woman of Samaria mentioned in the Bible?

While I was preoccupied with such matters of the heart, poor Mehmet Ali's worst fear came true: A summons arrived from the army. The ululations of a woman one morning bore the tidings. Such a howl, such a lament, as if someone had died. I dashed outside.

"Mehmet Ali! Mehmet Ali!"

There was no reply.

"Zeynep! İsmail!"

Again no reply. I ran in the direction of the howls.

"What's going on? What's all this about?"

That's what Mehmet Ali's wife was saying.

It seems unlikely to me that Mehmet Ali would've left without bidding me farewell.

The muhtar, two men from the gendarmerie, and Mehmet Ali were gathered in front of the door of the muhtar's house, along with a couple other men who'd also been drafted. Mehmet Ali's face was ashen. He looked in my direction but didn't seem to recognize me.

When I drew nearer to ask him what was amiss, he looked down, his expression morose and bitter.

Gesturing toward the muhtar and gendarmes, he mumbled, "I told you now, didn't I? I told you . . ."

The muhtar, seated between the men from the gendarmerie with the officious airs of a bureaucrat, was studying the stamped, printed documents he'd been handed, scrutinizing each page.

When he saw me, ceremoniously he rose to his feet, motioning for the gendarmes to do the same. Pulling up a chair, I sat down among them, whereupon I learned that the gendarmes would be visiting twenty-two more villages.

Mehmet Ali and the other draftees had received orders to be in Eskişehir within a period of twenty-four hours, no later.

Pointing in my direction, Mehmet Ali snapped, "Just ask the gentleman here. We could never make it in time!"

Never before had I seen such defiance in him.

Drawing on all of his official "authority," the muhtar coolly replied, "And why not? Of course you'll make it."

Mehmet Ali was fuming.

Just then Zeynep Kadın appeared. Standing with her feet planted firmly on the ground, she glared at everyone in the group. She was like a female wolf prepared to defend her cub to the bitter end.

More women started arriving. First one, then two, then five, their ranks swelling with each passing moment, murmuring to one another as if conspiring in sedition.

I turned to Mehmet Ali and said, "Your country needs seasoned soldiers like you. If you don't go fight on the front lines today, tomorrow the battle will be on your doorstep. I've said it time and time again. The enemy draws near. And this is different from the war you knew before. The people are fighting. Of their own free will. I can assure you it won't last long. It will be over in a single battle."

Zeynep Kadın cut in, "Fine but this is when we need our men the most. It's always like this. When work needs to be done, they come in and take our children away from us."

"Don't fret," I said. "While I may not be very useful myself, I'll hire on a workhand and make sure he sees to all that needs to be done."

Zeynep Kadın shrugged off my comment. But my words appeared to have had some effect on Mehmet Ali. While he may not have cut the figure of the fiercest of warriors, he suddenly took on the demeanor of a steadfast soldier, reminding me of the private I'd once known. He struck me as being more amenable than a moment ago, more tractable, and the officer within me began to stir.

"I wish," I said, "that they'd drafted me and I could go too." I spoke those words with such conviction that the eyes of Mehmet Ali and the other recruits gleamed.

One of them said, "With the help of God we'll rout the enemy. But I've heard we don't have any guns or ammunition."

In the heart of the Anatolian villager, feelings of positivity and realism have been vanquished by their other emotions. Once in a great while there is a spark of lyricism, but it glows but for the briefest of seconds. In his eyes, a man of great enthusiasm and a madman are one and the same. If you want to win his trust, you must be quiet, grave, and somber.

I collected myself.

Mehmet Ali left. I'd thought his departure would leave his household in shambles but nothing of the sort happened. They didn't even kiss each other's cheeks or embrace.

His sisters were silently weeping. Once or twice his wife almost started crying as well but Mehmet Ali shot her such a dark look that she swallowed back her tears like stones.

Zeynep Kadın was leaning against a wall. İsmail was standing beside her, his hands tucked into his sash.

Before he left, Mehmet Ali bowed before me and kissed my hand. Although it seemed he wanted to say something, he trudged off, his satchel slung over his shoulder.

Knowing that he may never return, I walked along behind him, a heaviness in my heart. He stopped to bid farewell to the people he came across on the road.

Were there tears in his eyes? Were his eyes the slightest bit moist? I don't know. Despite the differences between us, he was the only friend I had in the world. Hadn't he been the only person who helped me find a new direction in my life, which had been cleft in twain?

Who among my classmates, colleagues, and bookish friends had offered to lend a hand? They were all mired in their own troubles. Only Mehmet Ali had said, "Come with me to my village. Here in the city you're all alone."

My heart ached as I recalled those words. As I stood there, I felt a desire to howl like a jackal at the top of my lungs.

Mehmet Ali went down the hill and crossed the river. Along with the three other conscripts from the village, he walked through the fields. Not once did they turn to look back, perhaps because they thought it wouldn't be manly to do so. *Maybe*, I thought, *they'll be nameless heroes in a Turkish victory tomorrow. Maybe* . . . Regardless, as those four silhouettes shrank and shrank into the distance, they looked like four children walking to school in the morning.

*

Zeynep Kadın hasn't said a word since Mehmet Ali left. Her face as expressionless as a mask, she sits staring blankly at nothing.

But one day she said to me, "They took my baby while that lout is hiding out in the arms of that woman in her bed."

I asked who she was talking about.

"That Cennet woman, that's who. Took this guy in. A stranger at that, and a deserter. For ten days he's been hiding out at Süleyman's place. She cooks for him. Takes him into bed at night."

"In front of Süleyman?"

"That's how they sleep. She's got one of them on the right, the other on the left."

I couldn't help but laugh. But the oddness of the sleeping arrangement wasn't what bothered her.

"I'm going to report him. Afraid he's going to bring us trouble."

That's not exactly how Mehmet Ali's mother speaks. Every sentence she utters, always in the thickest of Anatolian accents, falls from her mouth as knotty and prickly as a briar.

For a long time now Süleyman has been the sole focus of my curiosity and interest. Delving down to the last detail, I imagine those scenes of fornication which Zeynep Kadın only sketches in the roughest terms.

The eternal struggle between men and women has never played out in more spectacular fashion. In this place, women and all the baser human instincts are roused, evocative of a predatory creature. There is the husband, who is like the carcass of a beast of prey sucked dry of blood and cast by the wayside, and then there is love, that immutable, invincible force of nature which is forever blind and blundering.

Whenever poor Süleyman tried to speak up, he either found his rival looming before him like a boulder or he was met with the mocking laughter of his wife, which is more dreadful than the roar of a tigress.

Hearsay reconfirmed my speculations. It seems that at one point Süleyman wanted to rough up his unwelcome guest but they scoffed at him. Another time the deserter knocked Süleyman to the ground with a blow from his elbow. When he charged at Cennet, however, she shoved him in the chest with both hands and bellowed, "If you so much as touch me, I swear I'll leave this very instant!"

That threat of leaving ... According to rumor, afterwards Süleyman did nothing but cower under the blanket at night, sobbing.

The situation became unbearable for the villagers. One day Bekir Çavuş saw Cennet at the fountain. Grinding his teeth, he stormed up to her and snarled, "Send that bastard packing or else!"

As coolly as a statue of Diana, she replied, "Or else what? What are you going to do?" Everyone thought that Bekir Çavuş was lusting after Cennet. Shaking his head, he walked away.

Another day the muhtar pounded on Süleyman's door. "Tell that scoundrel to leave!" he ordered. But his words fell on deaf ears. "We'll go," Cennet said, "but only if my husband divorces me." Süleyman, however, had no intention of divorcing his wife. The villagers decided that the only way to put an end to this scandal was to raid their home. They asked the imam, "If we catch them in the act, will that mean they're divorced in the eyes of Islam?"

"Of course," he replied.

One night after evening prayers the village notables got together. The imam was among the men. There was no ruckus or tumult; if İsmail hadn't come running to tell us, we never would've known anything was happening.

He said, "I went to get some water. That's when I heard about it." I saw a group of men walking from the mosque in the direction of Süleyman's home, and I went over to join them. When they reached his place, the imam rapped on the door three times with his cane. There was no reply.

Bekir Çavuş called out, "Süleyman! Open up." Again, silence. They waited for a short while and then one of the men leaned into the door with his shoulder. It burst open and everyone rushed inside, including me. In the commotion that ensued, I dropped the clay pitcher of water I was holding. "Heretics!" Cennet cried out. "Infidels!" The imam snapped, "*You* are the heretic here. You are the infidel. Out with you. You cannot stay here with Süleyman like this, sinning against God." I heard Süleyman shout, "Stop pushing me! Stop!" I don't know what happened afterward because I slipped away, fearing for my own safety.

I'd never seen İsmail in such a state of agitation. He was more overwrought than the day when his mother had beaten him. Pale-faced, he was panting for breath and his lips were trembling. Only when Zeynep Kadın stomped over to him and growled, "Why'd you drop the pitcher?" did he come to his senses.

Cennet and the deserter left the village early the next morning, and Süleyman was plunged into a lovelorn melancholy which began with weeping that rose up from the depths of his heart. Although he never shed a tear, he was constantly choked by sobs. Then he slipped into a dark silence. He neither ate nor drank, nor did he speak a word to anyone. For hours he would sit staring into nothingness.

The poor wretch had no one to console him except for Memiş, who never left his side. Without having to talk, the two madmen understood one another, somehow conveying across their silence earnest sentiments of the greatest import.

I wanted to know what they spoke about during those long, mysterious conversations.

After all, am I not also a madman like them?

Still, this tragedy of the heart brought new life to the stirrings of love in my imagination. Every two days or so I found myself traversing the road to Dulcinea's village, but in the heat of summer those journeys were exhausting.

Sometimes the trip was as laborious as crossing a desert. Beneath my feet the earth was searing hot and hard like the rocks spewed from volcanoes. I could feel the oppressive weight of the summer sky bearing down on me as if I was carrying the massive fiery orb of the sun on my shoulders.

"Why," I would ask myself, "do I go to the trouble? What's the point of this toil?" For a dream. For the shade of a wild flower. But is its scent alluring? Is it pleasing when pressed to the lips?

Come now, is every lover not a figment of our imaginations, a being fashioned and embellished in our minds? Whether she's a gentlewoman from the city or a village girl, we call her "my one and only."

I'd venture to say I've been smitten a few times in my life, and while my love was always the same, the women I loved were not. In that way, our hearts are like bees that suck nectar from every flower they come upon.

It wasn't for nothing that the mystic Eşrefoğlu said, "We are the bee, the honey is in us." That line makes quick work of the creature which poets are so fond of calling "the beloved."

In this regard Don Quixote is quite similar to the mystics of the Orient. Was humanity's greatest and most profoundly idealistic "character" not bound by the heart to a village girl for years on end? Whenever he chanced upon her, did he not treat her with the same refinement reserved for noblewomen?

Sancho could make no sense of his sire's misguided ways. "Is this," he asked, "what you call a princess, a lady of a castle? No, worship. This stinkpot with calloused hands is naught but a common village girl."

Regardless, Don Quixote bowed to the ground to kiss her hand. Turning to Sancho, he said, "Ah, such a wondrous scent. What a divine creature she is!"

Now I'm no different than Don Quixote going to see his Dulcinea, and I don't feel an ounce of shame for doing so. I walk. And the more I walk, the more my heart swells with excitement. The parched ground crackling under my feet is the plushest of green grass.

At times I pass by fields of crops, which in my eyes are beds of roses. In truth, the crops planted on those desolate fields yellowed before growing a few hands-breadth high, and the drooping ears of grain are testimony to a tale of misery rising up from the depths of the earth.

Ahead of me are always more bare hillocks. Undulating waves of dust.

But the orchestra within me transforms them into embellishments so enticing that they are even beyond the reach of the imagination. Soon I'll be by Dulcinea's side.

*

I had a hunch today. Sure enough, I saw her as soon as I stepped into the thicket of trees. She was hanging up the clothes she'd just washed. Her sleeves were rolled up and I saw that her arms were pure white as she hung the dripping clothes on some branches.

When she saw me, again she darted away like a wild deer. Again she hid among the trees. Again she kept glancing back . . .

No matter what happens, my fawn, today I won't let you slip away.

"Why do you keep running away?"

I walked toward her. She'd run in the opposite direction from her village, meaning that she wouldn't be able to escape so easily.

"What's to be afraid of? Stop, I won't bring you any harm."

As I spoke those words, I was still walking in her direction. She stopped and crouched down behind a tree. I took a few steps closer.

"Why are you scared of me? There's no need to be frightened."

"Don't, please. Don't."

"What do you think I'm going to do? Relax, go on with what you were doing. I'm just going to sit down for a bit."

"No, you can't. My aunt will see."

"What's your aunt going to see?"

"No, no, my aunt will see. You really can't."

She spoke these words in such a plaintive, pleading voice . . . Like an animal caught in a trap. She sounded like she was on the verge of tears. I stepped yet closer. There was only one tree left between us.

"Set aside your fears. I'm no stranger. You've seen me many times before. Did I ever do anything bad to you?"

She was trembling like a wet cat. Out of nervousness, perhaps? Or maybe common carnal excitement? I thought this because her voice was softening, becoming more and more like the mew of a kitten.

"No, no, my aunt will see."

My heart pounding in my ears, I knelt down beside her.

*

For no apparent reason Salih Ağa started a quarrel with Zeynep Kadın over a field they'd been cultivating for years, even back in the times when Mehmet Ali's father was around, claiming it as his own. Racked by sobs, she told me about the situation the other night. This woman who hadn't shed a tear since her son had been drafted into the army was now weeping because she might lose a plot of land. The strange thing was that the cost of leasing the field was included in the payments that I made. And now Salih Ağa was a claimant against me.

"There's nothing to fear. I won't give him anything. If need be, we'll take it to court."

She started crying even more.

"Court? No, please, not the court . . ."

"But why?"

"The ağa will pay them off. He and the judge will make a deal, and he'll try to take our other fields too."

"How could he do such a thing? Don't you have the title to the land, a record?"

"No, I don't have a thing. Nothing at all!"

"Then we'll call in witnesses."

"All of them would side with the ağa . . ."

I now understood why she was so upset. Fuming, I decided that I would speak to Salih Ağa myself.

And so I did. But what good did it do? None at all. Salih Ağa is like an automaton. While he appeared to possess all of the characteristics particular to living creatures, he neither listened nor spoke, and I didn't see a flicker of comprehension in his eyes. I got the impression that my mouth and his ears were separated by a distance of many miles.

Uncontrollably I started gesturing with my one hand and shouting. At one point, however, I looked up and saw that he'd sauntered away, so I ran after him, finally catching up with him in front of his house. Fixing his metallic eyes on me, he asked with a vague smile, "What's it to you?" and then he slipped through the door of his house, closing it behind him. Salih Ağa is quite like a weasel that dashes into its burrow at the first sound of approaching footsteps. And as he flees, your instincts for the hunt snap awake, giving you the urge to take aim.

I decided that the next best course of action would be to see the muhtar, but when I knocked on his door, I was told that he wasn't at home—a claim the veracity of which I doubted very much. As I was striding back home, anger unvanquished, I came across the imam.

"Imam Efendi, what do you think about what Salih Ağa is doing?"

"What's he doing?"

"He's trying to lay claim to poor Zeynep's land."

Bowing his head, the imam lapsed into silence and started stroking his beard.

I proclaimed, "It's insufferable. I'm going to speak with the district governor, the governor of the sanjak, and if need be, the provincial governor himself! Tell Salih Ağa I said so. He should open his eyes to the reality of the situation."

"Very well," the imam muttered, shuffling away.

As of today, Salih Ağa and I are officially at odds. It appears that in all my fury and ferocity, I am on the constant offensive, while he, resorting to feigned incomprehension, silence, concealment, and evasion, is beating a retreat. I get the feeling, however, that we are surrounded on all sides and a cloud of noxious gas hangs in the air.

*

"There's nothing to fear, Zeynep. I'm going to defend you until the very end."

Skeptically she shakes her head.

"I can only hope. We'll see . . ."

"Why are you so afraid? Aren't the crops mine? I am going to harvest them. And why shouldn't I? They're mine to harvest. And I'll do the same next year, without asking him. If he wants to go to court, so be it."

She winces when I say the word "court."

*

One night I was awoken by heart-rending screams. Leaping out of bed, I ran in the direction of the sound. It turned out that Mehmet Ali's wife was giving birth in the back room.

I asked Zeynep Kadın, who was standing next to the door, "Did you call for a midwife?"

"Why would I? I tied a rope to the beam. She'll hold onto that and get through just fine."

"And afterward?"

"Afterward what? We all give birth this way." Without another word she stepped into the room.

Oblivious to what was happening, İsmail was curled up fast asleep by the front door, deaf to the cries that had awoken me on the other side of the house.

The woman's screams were now an almost inhuman shriek. I lit a cigarette and started pacing in my room. A feeling of despair surged through me. It was more powerful than the anguish that had gripped me on the first night I arrived in the village.

I was like a man stuck on a small ship that was being thrown against the rocks, its sails in tatters.

The cries of Mehmet Ali's wife were the howling of the storm. We're going down. We're going down.

An abrupt scream and then silence. A profound silence . . .

That's when she must've given birth.

As of yesterday Mehmet Ali has a son. I didn't see the baby but İsmail told me that it's so small and light that you can carry it around in the palm of your hand and hardly even notice it's there.

"İsmail, I'm sure you were like that when you were born too. And look, you've stopped growing."

"If I get married, I'll grow more."

"You? Get married? İsmail, that's preposterous."

"Why? I've been engaged for three months. If the harvest is good, I'll get married for sure."

"You're not even fifteen yet, and you can't grow a mustache or a beard. Take care of growing up a bit first."

I could tell he was angry. Holding his head high and puffing out his chest like a turkey, he said, "She wants to be with me."

With great difficulty I held back my laughter.

"What about her parents?"

"She lives with her aunt 'cause she's an orphan. And if her aunt won't let us get married, I'll steal her away."

"Now look, you don't want to turn out like Süleyman do you? You've seen for yourself what happened to him."

I forgot to mention that Süleyman disappeared a few days ago. No one knows where he is, not even his friend Mad Memiş, who, when I asked him, merely pointed toward a vague point in the distance and grunted, grinning meaningfully.

The truth of the matter, however, requires no explanation. Everyone knows what Süleyman set out to find.

*

The crops have started wilting. Poor, miserable crops . . . Standing no higher than a two-year-old child, they seem to embody the torment of the soil of central Anatolia. At dusk, orphaned heads of grain droop on their stalks, gazing down at doleful roots clutching the earth.

As I look out over that landscape, I better understand why the Turks of old longed to press on toward Rumelia.

The heart of the motherland is a barren country consisting of salt lakes and chalky earth. The Turkish people here are reminiscent of Benjamin in the desert. Now they are encircled by a ring of hell and all of the rich, fertile lands have been wrested from them, which inspired the slogan of the War of Independence: "We'll either die or save ourselves."

There is no middle ground. The Turks will either break through the siege or give up their lives trying.

To give up one's life . . . Who has ever been asked to make such a sacrifice? But there are people among us who are ready and willing. I read about it in the Istanbul newspapers the other day. For all intents and purposes, the Treaty of Sèvres has been settled and hence so has Turkey's destruction. The government of Damat Ferid Pasha has dispatched three dignitaries to sign the treaty, one of whom is Rıza Tevfik. The very same Rıza Tevfik who introduced us to the delights of Turkish folklore. Why did he stoop to such treachery and betrayal? Why did he not instead join a troupe of old shamans and travel these lean lands, singing of the suffering of the people?

Oh, unhappy country! What a shame for those who don't know

how to love you. What a shame for those who love you yet are afraid to give up their lives in that silent tragedy of yours . . . The stones and earth offer an infinite bounty of patience and perseverance! In your bosom one either attains the peaks of epic heroism or learns to embody the abnegation and humility of the divinest saints.

If I were to cry out beneath the branches of that willow, Yunus Emre would speak to me:

> *The dervish must have a heart of stone,*
> *Eyes that well up with tears, and*
> *A gait slower than that of a lamb.*

Yes, my sage. Yes, my master. That is what I am trying to become here. But what is the meaning of this destitute state of nature? The sparse stunted crops, drooping ears of wheat, clammy willow leaves, stagnant water . . . What does it all symbolize?

In a setting like this, is the soul not a seed buried in the soil? I, reserve officer Ahmet Celâl, Ahmet son of Celâl Pasha, have become such a seed on the banks of the Porsuk River. I await the grace of God so I can drive my tendrils into the dark earth, send my buds out into the light, and bear fruit on my spreading branches. I can feel in my body the anguish of the earth in which I'm buried. I plunge myself into it.

I, Ahmet son of Celâl Pasha, who was born in one of the most majestic mansions in Istanbul, spread my wings and flew toward glimmering fantastical climes, only to plummet to the ground here with a broken wing. A soldier retired at the age of thirty-two, a crippled youth whose entire future now lies in the past . . .

"What are you doing?"

Ha! What does it matter . . .

*

It's clear to me that I haven't yet descended from the realm of thought and imagination. When I was leaving Istanbul, I'd decided that the source of the misery that tormented me was none other than my own mind, and I was determined to break free of it. Bidding farewell to metaphysics and rumination, I was going to live the life of a villager, becoming one of them in the process. But I can see now that I'm like a droplet of olive oil in a bowl of water, always floating at the surface, always separate. Perhaps that is why they call people like me the mainspring of society.

But are Turkey's intellectuals truly the mainspring? If that is indeed the case, then shouldn't I carry within me the Salih Ağas, Bekir Çavuşes, İsmails, and Zeyneps of society? As I've said, I feel closer to the animals here than the people. Untainted by loathing, I can love them with compassion, and my feelings find their mark. In particular the donkey has gotten used to me being around. Probably that's because I throw my arm over its neck and scratch its head for hours on end. At times like that the donkey looks up at me ever so sweetly, and sometimes it even follows me around when I go for a walk.

İsmail, on the other hand, is just as distant and cool as the first night I met him, although I've always reached out to him with friendship and love. I give him my old clothes. Once in a while I slip him some money. But none of my acts of kindness have succeeded in drawing him closer.

The other day I caught Zeynep Kadın complaining to someone about me on her doorstep. It would seem that I meddle in all of her affairs and that I stirred up trouble between her and Salih Ağa. Ever since I showed up, she said, the household has sunk further into poverty. Mehmet Ali was drafted into the army. A dispute arose about that plot of land. Now spoiled, İsmail refuses to do as he's told.

I was just about to go out when I overheard the conversation. Silently I tiptoed away from the door and slipped back into my room. Now, as I sit holding my head in my hands, I wonder:

Sure, I could act like them, talk like them, dress like them, and eat and drink like them . . . But how can I *think* like them? How can I *feel* the way they feel?

I consider burning all the books that fill my room.

Tearing down the paintings hanging on the walls and stomping on them.

Still, what good would it do? They've all become a part of me, indelibly and inescapably. The traces they've left cannot be scrubbed away. The walls of my internal self are lined with the paintings, drawings, signs, colors, and hieroglyphs of a stranger. So what would be the point of changing my outer façade? The real "I" has become something industrial in nature, chemical perhaps, kneaded into being by materials and elements brought from the outside world.

The other day while strolling on the plain I stumbled across an empty tin can. I stopped to look at it. The label was in English. A product of America most likely. I wondered who could have possibly left it there, and when. Driven by a strange sense of curiosity, I leaned down and picked it up, feeling like I was seeing something quite familiar from the distant past.

In these lands, I am the counterpart of that tin can.

*

Analogies, metaphors . . . Analogies, metaphors . . .

In life, however, such things aren't real. Life and reality exist in Salih Ağa's feet; life and reality exist in Zeynep Kadın's wrinkles; life and reality exist in the muhtar's grizzled beard; life and reality exist in İsmail's round eyes.

When the villagers—men, women, and children—return home from the fields, dreams flee from the branches of the willow under which I sit, scattering in fear. As these people, muddied in the course of their back-breaking labors, shuffle back to their mudbrick homes in large groups, in twos and threes, or alone, I feel stranger than usual, more thoughtless, useless, and meaningless.

These people of clay walk in silence. Some of them carry bundles of sticks on their backs, while others shoulder burlap sacks. Yet others carry baby goats, and some drive water buffalo before them. Head bowed, the donkey plods behind İsmail, taking short steps. Most of the women carry babies in slings across their chests, and the babies' heads loll as they doze. The little children who can walk on their own stay in the village, and they clamber over the heaps of garbage toward the people returning from the fields.

This scene is straight from the times before Noah, but tonight no signs of reward or punishment will appear in the sky. Darkness will fall as usual and Zeynep Kadın will step into my room with a dirty tray bearing a bowl of food she cooked with her daughters and daughter-in-law.

*

As I lie here, I can see small mounds of chaff. The village is about half an hour away. Nearby is Bekir Çavuş's field, in the middle of which his blind daughter is sitting alone. Her long hair shimmers like corn silk under the noontime sun. She's only about twelve or thirteen years old and so thin that you can count each of her ribs if you run your hand down her back. I can't help but wonder why they left her there by herself. They must have forgotten about her. And she probably thinks that everyone is still working the fields.

I decide to get up and walk her home but at that moment Salih Ağa's hunchbacked son comes lumbering impishly toward her. The kid reminds me of a lame goat. I say "kid," but he's probably in his teens, and he's got a voice that's deeper than that of a grown man.

Stopping in front of her, he says something, and she looks up at his face as if she can see him. The hunchback stands there, his hands tucked into the sash around his waist. After glancing around, he murmurs something else to her, whereupon she shyly bows her head. He takes off his conical hat and scratches his head for a while, and then he sits down beside her so that they're shoulder to shoulder.

But he can't sit still. First he tickles the back of her neck with a piece of straw, or maybe a thorn, and then he sets about trying to tickle the soles of her feet with his fingertips. Annoyed, she gets up to walk away but he grabs her by the arm and pulls her back down.

Never in my life have I seen anything so grotesque. This is not the case of your typical mischievous young man pestering a demure girl, but something monstrous . . . Like a snake trying to swallow a frog, or a gigantic spider spinning its web around a moth.

The hunchback is obviously hurting her now, because I can hear her crying out. I decide to put an end to this torment but now she's on her feet, dashing across the field as if she can see, and he's chasing after her.

When she stops at the bank of the river, once again she falls into her pursuer's clutches. The hunchback grabs her by the waist and starts pulling her into the water.

As I sit back down, I understand it all.

Human beings truly are the vilest of animals.

*

Salih Ağa went through with his intentions. Under the cover of night, he made off with what he considered to be his share of the harvest from Zeynep Kadın's field of crops. When I found out, I flew into a rage. I've never beaten a man, but that day I was determined to give that village ağa a sound thrashing, despite the pleading and protestations of everyone in the household, particularly Zeynep Kadın.

They tried to dissuade me, saying that Salih Ağa had informed them of his decision a few days earlier. And while I knew he'd laid claim to a portion of the harvest, I never expected him to take his brash insolence so far.

Very well, what's done is done. But how to proceed?

I'm not bothered in the least by my own losses. I'd only had a bit of corn planted, as well as some wheat, simply for the sake of helping out Mehmet Ali's family. But they seem quite distraught. Trying to quell my anger, they plead, "Thank you, but please let's not start a quarrel over this." What infuriates me is their fear and refusal to take action. I try to instill in them a sense of justice, but it's pointless. They are as apathetic as stones.

Having not yet developed into social beings, the inhabitants of this village live like cavemen. In those times, armed with an ax the strongest of the tribe would overpower everyone, stealing the food from their mouths and their wives from their dens, and the people accepted that as a given, like the forces of nature.

It is said that the villager prizes the notion of ownership above all else. Centuries of foreign invasions and local banditry, however, have dulled that sensibility in the denizen of the Turkish village. He carries within himself the timorousness of a herd of sheep cowering in the wake of a celestial calamity. But why is he afraid?

That is difficult to explain and equally opaque to analysis. Is it the brutal harshness of the natural environment that has driven the villager of Anatolia to such a state? Only the spirit of an orphaned child has any chance in these lands, which are as listless as the bosom of a callous stepmother.

All these philosophical ruminations, however, could do nothing to stop me from confronting Salih Ağa. I spotted him sitting in front of the coffeehouse. Slowly I approached, and his face blanched when he saw me.

"Did you steal our crops the other night?"

Head bowed, he refused to answer.

"Tell me, are you the thief? I swear, I'm going to drag you off to the police."

He took hold of his big toe.

"Tell me," I said. "Speak up."

I lost control and grabbed him by his shirt. He tried to lurch backwards but I held on tight, shaking him. Then he got to his feet, twisting and writhing in an attempt to break free. There was no one else around; the owner of the coffeehouse had probably gone to fetch some water. Salih Ağa thrashed in my grip like a jackal caught in a trap.

I felt his teeth on my hand. Like an animal, he was trying to bite me. The moistness of his black, sparse teeth on my skin transformed my rage into revulsion, and I shoved him so hard that he fell to the ground. In an instant, however, he was back on his feet and, leaping over the coffeehouse bench, he ran off.

For a while I stood there looking at the shoes of my adversary lying on the ground, unsure if I wanted to burst out laughing or break down in tears.

Why, I asked myself, had I taken everything so seriously? Why had I given myself over to such anger? For days I was tormented about the incident, and I even considered asking Salih Ağa for his forgiveness.

He, however, didn't seem to bear a grudge against me. Now that he'd gotten what he wanted, nothing else mattered. In fact, I got the impression he was pleased that the matter had been settled with such little fuss. Perhaps he even felt a certain disdain, seeing me as nothing more than an immature, impudent youth.

*

When the collector of the harvest tax came to the village one day, Salih Ağa was the first to meet him, and they sat for a while in conversation. Later they were joined by Bekir Çavuş, the muhtar, and the imam. Speaking with grave earnestness, Salih Ağa played the role of a man of great importance. As I walked by, they all rose to greet me, including Salih Ağa, so I approached them.

"Greetings, gentlemen."

The tax collector, a rotund grey-haired man, was wearing a single-breasted suit with a rubberized collar. He was sitting with his knees pressed together. Occasionally he nodded off as the men talked.

"But this year has seen some bad luck . . ."

"What are you saying? Bad luck?"

"God willing, it will all work out fine."

Thus I found myself in the middle of a discussion that had neither beginning nor end. I should note, however, that the topic changed when I joined them, as did the men's expressions, with the exception of the tax collector, who remained as groggy as before. For fifteen days he'd been on the road, travelling all the way from Sivrihisar. "That's why," he said, "I can't answer your questions about what's happening in the country. You're closer to Ankara anyways."

We're closer to Ankara . . . For some reason, that idea cheered my heart. One day I will go to that bustling city. I have my hesitations, however. Not because I'm uneasy about the prospect of being at loose ends, but because I wouldn't want to be an unproductive visitor to the new capital.

"Have any of you ever been to Ankara?"

It turned out that only the tax collector had been there.

"I spent some time in Kalecik before I was appointed to Sivrihisar. About two weeks, while I was passing through. It's not a bad place, except there's no water or trees. And it's so expensive, incredibly expensive . . ."

Bekir Çavuş said he'd recently travelled as far as Polatlı.

"I saw the trains," he said. "They're full of soldiers going to Eskişehir. And on the way back to Ankara, they're loaded with supplies."

The muhtar cut in, "All the bigwigs are there."

Yet again the tax collector stirred himself awake. "Bigwigs?" he mumbled. "True, very true. My supervisor is in Ankara. I've been there . . ."

I asked, "Sir, are the salaries paid on time?"

"The salaries," he replied, "have never been paid in a more orderly fashion. On the thirtieth of every month the payrolls are drawn up. All you have to do is sign the paperwork and it's done."

My heart swelled with pride upon hearing of the efficiency of our government.

"Everything depends on that . . . On my journey from Kalecik to Ankara, I was entrusted with a sum of two thousand lira. We had to walk much of the way and sleep out in the open. Praise be to God, we had no trouble. All the roads are safe."

My heart swelled with pride again. I felt as if I personally had been in charge of ensuring the protection of public order. Gesturing toward the villagers seated around us, I said, "They say nothing is going well. All they talk about is ill luck and bad harvests."

The tax collector didn't hear me, however, as he'd nodded off again.

Tracing a large circle with this finger over the ground, one of the villagers said, "Don't talk like that. Back in the old days we used to have grain pots all around here filled with barley. Open them now and you'll see they're all empty."

At that moment the tax collector opened one of his eyes and gestured as if to say, "He's lying. Don't believe a word he says."

While the granaries of the Anatolian villager are empty, the Turkish intellectual is waging war against seven different countries. In Istanbul, journalist and would-be politician Ali Kemal calls this madness, but I see it as part of a lofty and inspiring panorama.

The Ankara-based newspaper *National Sovereignty* has started running a column called "Disgraces of the Entente Forces in Istanbul" and it published an article titled "Victors, Come to Your Senses." At the same time, the slogan "sovereignty of the people" has been spreading like a revelation, even stirring me awake here in my seclusion. The name Mustafa Kemal shines in Turkey's dark skies like a morning star, around which other stars are appearing. People are talking about the Turkish army. Mehmet Ali sent a letter in which he said that his regiment is stationed in Kütahya. Once in a while Turkish troops and officers pass through, and I host some of them here in the village.

No trace is left of those officers I knew from the Great War. While I know some of them, they are changed men, more like the leaders of a new order than humdrum heads of regiments. During the Great War, they were weary in mind and soul, always complaining about one thing or another, and they were quick to criticize the policies of the government. Now, they refuse to tolerate debates. "Victory will be ours," they say.

Alarmingly, however, I find myself surrounded by people who do nothing but quibble. Are such villages, these outposts of illness, poverty, and despair, not our one and only source of strength? Are the gaunt, cowardly, dull-eyed ghosts among whom I live not the men that these officers are supposed to lead into war?

*

The other day I saw how the troops are transporting munitions to the front. A long caravan of squeaking and creaking ox carts . . . What a sorrowful sight! Some of the oxen were so emaciated that their haunch-bones had torn through their skin, leaving open wounds that were infested with flies. And the men in the caravan were like giant insects themselves; there was nothing human about them, not in form, gait, nor voice. The carts, which have two wheels and are hitched to the yokes of the oxen with long poles, appeared to be extensions of the bodies of the drivers. That is where they sleep and keep their bedding, blankets, rations, and water. Difficult as it may be, the shell of a tortoise can be pried from its back, but those carts are inseparable from the men driving them.

Plying the endless roads of Anatolia, those peculiar cart-creatures plod mournfully along, crossing rivers, traversing hills, and winding their way among outcrops and thickets of briars. Along with the worn-out wares of Turkish villagers, you are also carrying the wares of epics toward a battlefront unlike any other, and that is why, as I gaze upon you from a distance, I see you as mythological beings.

Surely the Turks of old who travelled in great waves of migration and conquest were followed by similar caravans. The possessions of Attila the Hun may very well have been thus transported, and when the Oghuz tribes spread across Anatolia, they too were probably accompanied by such creaking of wheels. I have little doubt that traces of these strange, sorrowful carts have been scored as fossils into the flanks of ancient stones. But still, despite such historical flights of the imagination, people fail to find in them the stuff of legend.

As the carts pass by, I cling to hope for success in the war. Creak, screech, creak, screech . . . It's as if my spine is being sawn in half, and the weight of all those oxen suddenly comes bearing down on me like a dark nightmare.

The officers said, "Victory will be ours." The Battle of İnönü marks a turning point, does it not? In that clash, did the Turkish army not rekindle a tradition that had been lost for centuries?

"The rear of a battlefront is like the backstage of a theater." I can't remember where I read that line, but it rings true. A tragedy penned by the likes of Shakespeare or Racine will soon be brought to life as kings, queens, and the pomp and pageantry of a palace appear on stage. Beforehand, however, we see that preparations backstage are underway. There are sundry props made from tattered taffeta reeking of sweat and half-hungry stagehands come and go among them, squatting down and getting up.

The majestic scene about to be unveiled consists of those things.

*

These days I too have started getting angry with İsmail. He neither takes care of work nor sits still. He's become mischievous, so indescribably mischievous. Sometimes he disappears for hours on end, sometimes even days, and no one knows where he goes.

In the early days of his roguery, some rather momentous scenes played out. Flying into a rage, Zeynep Kadın would lay into him time and time again but in vain, as İsmail would emerge from those beatings as spirited as ever. Once he shook his fist at her as she was stomping toward him.

"Don't you dare," he snarled.

Zeynep Kadın was stunned.

"What did you say? What did you just say?"

"Don't you dare hit me," he said.

"My God, he's raising his hand against me!"

The spell that had held İsmail in check was now broken. His shell cracked open and a strange new creature slithered forth like a slug—mysterious, slick, and cynical. Its skin would tighten up when touched, and it would extend its antennae as it left your hand covered in slime.

He never used to smoke. Whenever I offered him a cigarette, he'd turn it down. But now, from dawn till dusk he filches cigarettes from the packs I keep on my desk.

One day I said, "If you want a cigarette, just ask and I'll give you one. But stop taking things from my room without asking."

He sauntered away without replying.

In the past, he was polite with me in his own way. Nowadays, however, he snubs me at every chance.

I'd like nothing more than to give him a good thrashing.

*

As of late, I keep coming across İsmail on the road to the village of the beautiful girl whose name I don't know. Either he's returning when I set out, or he's on his way there when I'm coming back.

I pretended not to see him once, and another time he pretended not to see me.

One day, however, we came face to face in the copse of poplars, and we had no choice but to acknowledge each other. Both of us, however, suddenly found ourselves strangely tongue-tied. Some crows were feeding on the carcass of an animal in the stream, which was running low at the time, and they flew off squawking and cawing when another flock of crows swooped in.

İsmail and I started walking. At one point we stopped, overcome by that unease particular to people in awkward situations, and we watched some of the crows fly off. Taking out my cigarette case, I lit a cigarette and offered one to İsmail.

"What's happening in that village?"

"Nothing. They're just working."

"Were you going to go back home?"

"Mm-hmm."

"Let's walk back together then."

We about-faced and started walking in the direction of our village. After about fifteen minutes of silence, without turning to look at him I asked, "Is your fiancée from there?"

He didn't reply.

"This is the fourth time I've seen you on this road. So I assume the girl you're in love with is from that village."

"As you say, sir."

"Tell me, which girl is she? I know just about everyone from around here."

"Emine. From the Şabangil family. She knows you."

"Emine . . ."

My heart started pounding and my mouth went dry.

"You must be mistaken. I don't know anyone named Emine."

But İsmail was adamant: "As I said, she knows you."

His voice was flat, devoid of anger or reproach.

"This Emine . . . Is she tall, with green eyes? Bright white teeth when she smiles?"

With a saucy grin he said, "Mm-hmm. That's her."

My ears started ringing.

"What did she say about me?"

"She said a guy missing an arm comes around."

"'A guy missing an arm'? What kind of thing is that to say?"

Lowering his eyes, he fixed his gaze on the right side of my body. Then he looked quizzically at me as if to say, "Well, *aren't* you missing an arm?"

Sometimes during moments of great agitation my missing arm starts to ache. That's precisely what happened as I stood there with İsmail. My non-existent arm was throbbing with pain.

I had an overwhelming desire to give that dwarf an all-mighty slap with my left hand.

*

My right side ached all night long and I didn't get a wink of sleep. The same unease that afflicted me when I first arrived in the village has come rushing back. I feel so strange and isolated. Once again the bleak map of the Anatolian plains has been etched into my mind, and I see myself as nothing more than a black dot affixed to a far-flung corner of this vast barren wasteland.

Here I suffer the same anguish that tormented me in Istanbul. Everything is conspiring against me: The stones, earth, water, people, animals . . . And I don't have the strength to fight back against all this antagonism. Constantly I'm being trod underfoot, again and again.

In that regard, İsmail seems so much more resilient than me. Nature twisted and transformed him until, even before he turned seventeen, his face was as wrinkled as that of an old man.

His spirit, which is a reflection of these harsh, rugged lands, is well-versed in the wiles of avenging itself on his enemies. Like a young gorilla that knows every inch of the jungle, he plucked the sweetest, most luscious piece of fruit around and, clutching his prize in his paws, sets about licking it.

What was the secret of his success? How could a fresh young woman endure such a bizarre, puckered freak of nature with rotting teeth?

Emine's white teeth gleam in the darkness as brightly as two rows of pearls. Will İsmail really make them his own? Lithe and alluring, she sways above me, a tender willow shoot. Is İsmail's body going to squirm up that branch like a caterpillar?

No, it can't be. Get down from there. Tomorrow I'm going to say to her, "Emine, open your eyes. You'll regret it later. That dwarf would never be a good husband for you. Have some pity on your youth and beauty."

But what if she says, "What's it to you?" Would I proclaim my love to a village girl in the debonair manner of the Istanbulite? Would such preposterous, pathetic behavior befit me? Could I bear it? *Come now*, I tell myself, *let them do as they will. They're just two villagers. Who cares if they get together and make love?*

Despite my attempts to console myself, sleep evades me. *My God, I'm jealous of İsmail. I, Ahmet, son of Celâl Pasha, am jealous of the runt brother of my erstwhile orderly Mehmet Ali, so jealous that I want to grab him by the neck and wring the life out of him.*

*

For days now I've been like a man in desperate search of a cure for a toothache. By busying my mind with the most inconsequential of matters and burying myself in books, I try to forget my pain.

Sometimes I go out and roam the countryside. I don't know if it's coincidence or mere habit, but more often than not I find myself in the environs of Emine's village, and then that ache starts throbbing again in all its brutal ferocity.

This isn't the first time I've been enamored of a woman. But it *is* the first time I've been confronted with an impossible love. How does one pick a wild rose hemmed in by thickets and thistles? I don't know. What should one say? What should one do? I'm at a loss. Should I chase her down like the hunchback pursued Bekir Çavuş's blind daughter? I'd like to go ask him.

There's only one person who can really enlighten me on the subject, however, and that's İsmail. If I could endure his face, I'd approach him. But I know what would happen. I'd ask, "What did you do to win Emine's heart?" and he'd merely reply with a smirk because he himself doesn't know what he did. It just happened of its own accord. True, there aren't any young men left in the villages and the girls—the virgin girls—are faced with the prospect of aging into spinsterhood, so İsmail's proposal of marriage must have held a certain appeal. Would she be able to find anyone better? After all, Mehmet Ali's family is fairly well off.

They own around twenty-five acres of land, and everyone is convinced that Zeynep Kadın has a stockpile of money. Emine is more or less an orphan living with her aunt, as her father was killed in the Balkan Wars and her mother got married again, leaving Emine behind.

I learned about the details of her life from Zeynep Kadın, who is vehemently opposed to İsmail marrying Emine. "I won't let him bring her around here if they get married," she says. "He can take her wherever he wants." Then she adds, "Then there's that hag of an aunt of hers. She's the one who caused all this trouble. She wants to palm off that buck-naked orphan on us."

When Zeynep Kadın said "naked," a tremor of delight ran down my spine. In my mind's eye, I began stripping Emine of the dirty, crude garments she wears as if I was peeling a thick-skinned fruit, imagining her pale skin. She has full breasts and thighs, and firm round shoulders. I've seen her long, graceful neck, so I'm certain she has a waist to match.

I say to Zeynep, "You have every right to put an end to it."

"But does he listen to me? Does he?"

He doesn't. In fact, the only thing he hasn't yet done is beat his mother.

"I wish Mehmet Ali was here. He'd fix things right."

"But I'm here, aren't I? I've told you time and time again that I can take care of everything he'd do."

She shot me a baffled glance, as if I were speaking sheer nonsense.

*

One evening I was sitting on the flat roof of the house. Bathed in the reddish-purple glow of the sky, I was lost in the mad meanderings of my imagination. İsmail came up and squatted down beside me.

"Got a cigarette?"

I held out the pack without looking at him.

That is the hour when the livestock start returning to the village. The hooves of the water buffalo descending the hills sound like the pounding of summer rain. Lambs bleat, awaiting their mothers' baa-baa replies, and then a donkey starts to bray. You can hear the clucking of chickens as they set about roosting in their coops and the howling of dogs in the distance.

Noah's Ark is beginning to fill . . . I wonder if the end of world is upon us. Every single night that notion consumes my thoughts, filling my heart with hopeful joy.

"What did you say to my mama?"

That was what İsmail asked me. I thought about how splendid it would be to lay him across an altar of stone and slice his throat in honor of this apocalyptic evening, just as Abraham had planned on doing to his son. After all, in the Quran was it not İsmail who was to be sacrificed?

I pretended that I hadn't heard him, but he went on mumbling beside me. Spinning toward him, I snapped, "What are you muttering about?"

He was so stunned by the harshness of my tone of voice that I almost laughed. His already small eyes shrunk to the size of nail-heads beneath his thick, furrowed eyebrows and his face became as wrinkled as a dried fig.

I looked away, but found no respite. His presence filled the air, weighing it down like quicksilver. A suffocating stench resembling dishwater, stables, and public toilets hung in the air like a cataclysmic cloud of gas, making my stomach turn. Ah, the human creature! So adept at turning nature into a murky cesspool. If it hadn't been for that boy beside me, if it hadn't been for that mud house, the clumps of worms writhing below, or the muck oozing from our food and drink, life on these arid undulating plains set aglow by the crimson evening sky could have been so much more pure and noble.

"You said . . ."

"I said that if you try to marry that girl, I'll drag you off by the ear and enlist you in the military."

His face turned ashen. In a trembling voice he asked, "Would they take me at this age?"

"If you're old enough to get married, you're old enough to join the army. That's the way of the world now."

Silently he slunk away like a whipped cat.

*

One question plagues my thoughts: Is Emine truly taken with the idea of marrying İsmail? One day I pulled her deep into the grove of poplars and asked, "Are you sure you want to marry him?"

She shrugged. And then with a laugh, she looked away and replied, "I don't know."

"If you don't know, who does?"

"My aunt." Before I could even tell her to stop, she dashed away as swift as a deer. I longed for nothing more than to catch her around the waist. There was something so feminine about the way she fled . . . My heart started pounding in my chest.

"Emine, wait. There's something else I want to tell you."

In fact, I had something to say, but who would listen? Even if she stopped, she wouldn't have understood a word I said. Still, I followed after her, not quite running but loping along, and the right sleeve of my shirt swung back and forth like an empty sack. I wondered if she'd burst out laughing if she turned around and saw me, so I stopped. Emine was now an indistinct shadow on the road to her village, drawing farther and farther away.

I slumped down beside the creek. There's an expression in *The Book of Dede Korkut*: To moan and bemoan. That's what I wanted—to moan and bemoan deep in my heart.

Where should I go?

Where do I belong?

With whom should I speak?

Who would understand me? Who could find a remedy for my woes? Who would be able to save me from this affliction and exile? What brother? What sister? What companion? Motherland, why are you so merciless, so unyielding? Why are you such a stranger to my suffering? Am I your stepchild? Or are you a stepmother to me? If I am your stepchild, for whose sake did I sacrifice my arm? At such a young age, why am I a human wreck on the bank of this creek?

After I gave up my youth for you, was it not me who burned with longing for you in that fallen city? Now I've come. I'm here. But your girls flee from me. They turn their backs. Whenever I hold out my hand, it's left hanging in the air.

If you truly were a stepmother, would your anguish so closely resemble mine? If you were like me, so strange, so destitute . . . Would you be this helpless, even without speaking in depth of your troubles? In my eyes, your face is one and the same with Zeynep's. So what prevents us all from understanding one another?

I sat crouching by the creek until evening as those thoughts spiraled through my mind.

The bare plains of Anatolia become even eerier at night. Under the golden mosaics of the sky's majestic dome, these dusky lands crumble away and vanish, disappearing so profoundly that it seems you must've slipped into nothingness long, long ago. Life exists in that vibrant, bustling, luminous realm up above, and it's as though one of those civilized cities has shifted around and now gazes contemptuously down on you. If my head wasn't spinning, I'd lie on my back until dawn observing that illuminated spectacle.

But my head *is* spinning. Did some giant grab me by the arm and hurl me to the moon? This place really is no different than the moon— just as lifeless, just as drab. Everything seems to have fossilized, and there's neither sound nor movement. If I move the slightest bit, it will all shatter into pieces. So be it . . . So be it.

*

In the village, preparations for winter are unending. The onions were dried and cured. The bulgur was pounded for days in mortars. The wheat was ground into flour, which was then used to make dozens of sheets of dough. Next it was time for the walnuts, heaps and heaps of them, and the stables were filled to the rafters with hay. In the meantime, the women have been smacking patties of fresh cow dung onto the outer walls of their houses. Zeynep Kadın's home has been covered from top to bottom with these bronze-colored medallions, much like the dignitaries under Sultan Abdul Hamid were decked out in medals. And what a stench! The entire natural world reeks of cow dung.

Along with her daughters and daughter-in-law, Zeynep Kadın has been working from morning until night. When they go out, they leave Mehmet Ali's baby son on the doorstep. Luckily for him, the area where they work is nearby, so when he starts crying, his mother can rush over to him. On numerous occasions I've kept him company at his daytime abode by the door. It occurred to me that human babies are much like a half-buried vine of the melon family, but when they move, they take on the appearance of a writhing mass of worms. Regardless of the perspective you take, however, they are more like products of the earth than a woman's womb.

The baby is so lacking in personality that they haven't named him yet. By post we asked Mehmet Ali for his opinion on the matter a few times but he never replied. Did he simply forget? He contents himself with writing, "Send my greetings to my offspring." So I've resorted to calling the baby "Nameless."

"Hey, Nameless. Nameless."

With great difficulty he turns his head, which is massive compared to his puny body, in my direction, and his expression is so mournful that it makes me want to weep. In all honesty, the child is a prime example of why Schopenhauer was right in his theory of bachelorhood. One glance at that poor creature is proof of the notion that bringing a child into the world is tantamount to murder.

"Hey Nameless, smile. Play a little."

Now on the verge of tears, he scowls and pouts. He's so unaccustomed to people spending time with him that my attentions are nothing short of torture.

Thrusting something into his hands to keep him occupied, I sit back and watch the workers.

People are more like ants than anything else. No other species displays such a knack for labor and economics. Combine that with an ability to think about the future, and they are raised above the level of animalism.

In this vile, unkempt corner of the world, why does this conglomeration of vulgar people inspire in me a feeling that borders on respect? Aren't they the same nobodies I scorn and scoff at day in and day out, and even loathe at times? But when, from a distance, I observe them toiling away, they appear to me as champions of a great cause.

I've seen those very same women dancing at weddings, but their movements were awkward and clumsy compared to the gracefulness with which they work. The way they swing their arms as they grind bulgur in the massive mortars, crouch and rise at the feeding troughs, and double over under the weight of sacks moves me as much as the rhythmic poses I've seen in the carvings of the ancient Greeks and Egyptians.

So much so that when Zeynep Kadın approaches me, I get the urge to kiss her hand.

*

The raw, biting winds of autumn are upon us. How they sweep across the bleak rolling plains of Anatolia . . .

Nothing is as ominous, horrific, or gloomy as the constant howling of that wind. Other calamitous events, such as a desert storm devouring a lost caravan, scores of owls overrunning the ruins of a town, the heart-rending cries of sailors sinking with their ship, the collapse of mountains, the eruptions of volcanoes, the roar of avalanches, and the surging of floods pale in comparison.

When the winds blow, I feel like one of Dostoyevsky's characters: An exile wandering the roads of Siberia, a vagabond on the streets of Moscow, or a criminal plotting his escape while lodging at an inn on the borderlands. A bitter pain starts to gnaw at my heart.

On one such windy night, I was lying in bed, tossing and turning. A chorus of howling dogs joined the roaring of the wind, making for a hellish concert, and I wondered if djinn and fiends from the underworld were out there dancing in the darkness.

Getting up, I peered out the window. The dogs were now barking even more wildly, which could only mean one thing: A stranger was approaching the village.

I listened intently, and soon enough I heard the sound of footsteps. Who could it possibly be, at this hour of the night? Still barking, the dogs gathered in front of the house. Opening the window and leaning outside, I shouted at them to quiet down, but the wind was blowing so violently that I feared for a moment that it would take off my head. Panting for breath, I backed away from the window. The dogs were now growling as if preparing to lunge in for an attack.

I sensed that whoever was out there had stopped when I called out. "Who's there?"

I heard a man's voice, but all I could make out was an "s" and an "l." Poking my head out the window again, I repeated, "Who's there?"

The voice was closer this time. "It's me, Süleyman."

In my groggy state, I didn't understand at first who this "Süleyman" was but then it dawned on me.

"What are you doing out there?"

Without replying, as silently as a shadow he started making his way toward his house. I closed the window, thinking that the way Süleyman suddenly appeared was like a corpse being washed ashore by a tempestuous sea.

I couldn't sleep all night. When the others woke up, I told them about the extraordinary events of the previous night. Zeynep Kadın appeared uninterested. İsmail, however, immediately dashed outside in the direction of Süleyman's home.

*

Here's what happened to Süleyman:

In search of Cennet, he travelled from village to village. I'm not sure where, but at one point he found her. She was with her lover at the time. At first, she pretended not to know him. When he insisted that she return home with him, however, she said, "Fine, but things don't work like that. Everyone knows about us. Your honor has been ruined. There's only one thing to do, and that's for you to divorce me. That way you're honor will be cleared. Then we can get married again."

Süleyman agreed to her terms, and they went to the nearest town, where he pronounced the triple talaq before the judge, thereby divorcing her. As they were leaving the court, he said, "Eh, I did what you wanted. Now let's go back to the village and get married."

Laughing, Cennet replied, "You don't understand a thing about sharia. Sure, you divorced me. But now I have to get engaged with someone else for a day before I can marry you again."

The "temporary" fiancé was at the ready: Her lover. And what did Süleyman do but personally hand her over to him and wait at their doorstep until the break of dawn, whereupon he knocked on their door. But there was no answer. After a while the lover opened the door and said, "What do you want?"

"I'm here to see Cennet Hanım."

"Cennet Hanım? What for?"

"She knows. We're going to go to my village."

"Like hell you are. She's my wife. Why would she go with you?"

But Süleyman persisted, determined as he was to wait for her. Shaking his fist in Süleyman's face, the lover snarled, "Stay the hell away from us, and don't stir up any trouble," whereupon Süleyman scuttled off. For weeks, however, he wandered around the village, hoping to get another chance to speak with Cennet. During the day he went from door to door, begging for food, and at night he slept in the fields. But not once did he see her.

So, what happened next?

Even Süleyman isn't sure. The most logical theory is that he had to return home because the townsfolk stopped giving him bread.

For the villagers here, the most tragic aspect of Süleyman's adventure was the fact that he'd been on the brink of starvation, which is why they started taking bowls of food to his house. He refused, however, to eat anything. His sole desire was tobacco, and all he did was sit around smoking cigarettes. While there was nothing particularly extraordinary or unusual about his behavior, he spoke of nothing except Cennet, and whenever the topic was raised, his eyes would gleam like black onyx.

He still clung to hope. He concluded every sentence by saying, " . . .but one day she'll return. She'll see she needs me and come back."

"You going to take her back in?"

Instead of replying, he'd stare blankly into the distance. When Süleyman first showed up, he had a bushy beard that lent him a certain air of grandeur, but when the village barber shaved it off, half of his newfound charisma vanished along with it. Slowly over time, he slipped into a monotonous routine and began leading a life bereft of all meaning. People stopped coming around to see him and, just as before, he was left with no one but Mad Memiş.

*

The most important events that transpired this winter can be summed up as follows:

In December, Mehmet Ali was given ten days of leave, so he came back to the village for a visit. He said his regiment was still stationed in Eskişehir. "Life's not so bad. Plenty of food and drink. The officers treat us good. They don't beat us and swear like they did before. But we're getting bored 'cause there's not much to do." He said that he saw Mustafa Kemal Pasha a few times at the train station, as well as İsmet Pasha. "What's Mustafa Kemal like? And what about İsmet? Go on, speak up!" All he could muster in reply was, "Well, a bit like this, a bit like that." I wished I could've have lent him my imagination, sensibilities, and tongue so he could describe in vibrant detail those two stars blazing in the twilit bosom of the homeland.

"What are Mustafa Kemal's eyes like? Is he tall, or short? What kind of expression did he have? How did he walk? What was he wearing?"

Mehmet Ali failed to answer any of those queries in his reply, which, as usual, was terse. "When we saluted him, he said, 'Greetings, soldiers!'"

While Mustafa Kemal's manner of addressing the troops was

fascinating, the description provided little in the way of particulars that the mind could use to conjure up an image of that great man.

"Does he have a deep, rich voice?"

"I couldn't hear him very well . . ."

"Well, you heard him say, 'Greetings, soldiers!' didn't you? So what was his voice like?"

Mehmet Ali becomes uncomfortable during such lines of questioning and usually tries to change the subject.

"They say the Greeks are going to attack again soon."

"Are you ready?"

"With God's help, we'll be ready, sir. But . . ."

But what? In order to explain situations of that sort, one must delve into the realm of general ideas, opinions, and observations, something which Mehmet Ali's mind is unaccustomed to doing.

In short, I gleaned nothing from Mehmet Ali during his stay, and he left as he'd come. As he'd come? Not exactly.

Before departing, he gave İsmail a sound beating with the hilt of his bayonet. But nothing could have demonstrated to me that beatings do nothing in the way of instruction and perhaps always have a negative effect. Afterwards, İsmail became unrulier than ever. Both at home and on the streets of the village, he was like a vicious beast. The expression in his eyes, which had always reminded me of the skittishness of a bird or rabbit, was now filled with wild fury. At times when he spoke with me, I got the impression he was nothing but a large field rat that had somehow learned how to talk.

Thankfully, our conversations were few and far between. I began to wonder, however, if he was harboring secret suspicions, and I couldn't shake off the feeling that he held a grudge against me. It would be best, I thought, if I found a new place to live. One day I discussed the issue with Bekir Çavuş.

"I've got a place," he said, "but it's a wreck."

"Couldn't it be fixed up?"

"Sure, but it'd cost a lot."

"How much?"

"Thirty or forty."

We went and looked at the place, which was just outside the village. It faced the mountain in the distance and had two rooms, beneath which was a stable. Outside the village . . . I was eager to set to work immediately.

"But who'll look after me?"

"Our kids. They've got nothing better to do."

I'd thought Zeynep Kadın would be upset when I told her. But she wasn't, not in the least, which suited me fine. I was so fed up with being at Mehmet Ali's house that I couldn't wait to move.

My new home, with its back turned to the village . . . Bekir Çavuş had been using it for storage, which explained the sturdy door and bars over the windows. I changed nothing about its external appearance and kept the barn, as I plan on getting a small donkey to keep me company. While I doze upstairs, it will patter around below, scratching at the earth with its front hooves. And when I find myself mired in cheerless thoughts, it will let loose with a heartbreaking bray as though aware of my misery, and I'll slowly make my way downstairs. Placing my arm around the donkey's downy neck, I'll gaze into its glossy black eyes and speak at length, baring my deepest secrets.

I'll never make it carry loads, nor will I burden it with a saddle. Every day I'll have it groomed, because it's a blessed creature. All the holy books revealed by God make mention of donkeys. And its face will be a thousand times more lovable than puny İsmail's.

Puny İsmail? Yet again I mention him. I have two problems. Salih Ağa is one, İsmail the other . . . Both are an incessant cause of torment.

I'm not counting the craggy ground, which makes me think of Zeynep's sullen face.

As winter draws ever nearer, I've found that I'm no longer shocked by the sight of the hunchback pursuing the blind girl, nor by the way he pulls her into unlocked barns to have his way with her. The imam performing his ablutions at the public fountain doesn't disturb me, nor does the way the muhtar smirks through his grizzled beard . . . I've grown used to them. Salih Ağa and İsmail are now the only source of vexation to which I cannot become accustomed.

*

Over the course of the winter, Süleyman and I became rather close friends, which was natural because he oversaw the repairs on my new home. He mixed the mortar while Memiş hauled the stones, and Arabacı Recep, the only craftsman in the village, took care of the carpentry. Nowadays I try to keep Süleyman by my side as much as I can, and sometimes we eat together. We enjoy a tranquil friendship . . . Hardly ever do we speak.

On numerous occasions when I've laid down in bed to rest, he sits on the floor cross-legged, and for hours we stay that way, neither of us feeling the need to speak a word. When the weather is pleasant, we go out for walks. One time I took him as far as Emine's village.

Since the incident with Cennet, Süleyman has become so thin that he is, in every sense of the expression, mere skin and bones. Whenever he leans down to pick something up or overexerts himself, I fear that his body will break in two with a loud crack. On the day when we walked to the other village, he collapsed upon our arrival at the thicket of poplar trees. I imagined that the bones of a skeleton suspended in the air would clatter to the ground in much the same way if the sinews holding them together snapped. For a long while he lay there, gasping for air, and I wondered if he was breathing his last.

"I'm okay," he said. "My heart gives me trouble sometimes. Give me a minute, it'll pass. This is why the army wouldn't take me."

I thought, *Maybe that's why Cennet didn't want you either.* When we're alone together, once in a while I broach the subject of Cennet. His eyes glisten and his gaunt frame becomes as taut as a drawn bow.

"Have you heard anything about her?"

"I heard she left him."

"So what's she doing now?"

"They say she's gone the way of the whore, but it's on their heads."

I think I was more distraught than him because he grinned and added, "I knew it would happen. She'll regret it all and come home."

"Will you take her back?"

He merely gazes at the ground in silence, suddenly unsure of himself.

In all truth, who among us is sure of themselves? We men are a miserable lot.

*

This winter the general expectation was that the muhtar's wife would die. But she didn't.

One evening before the nighttime prayer, the muhtar came pounding on my door. "Efendi, I brought you a news bulletin from town."

"Is it good news?"

"Here, read it. They say we won the war."

My hands trembling, I took the grimy, wrinkled piece of paper and held it up to the lamp. A second victory in İnönü . . . My heart leapt in my chest. As if I was reciting a poem, I sang the words to myself as I read the bulletin line by line.

"You see?" I said, turning back to the doorway, but the muhtar had already shuffled off to the mosque. I was choked up with emotion. It's part of the human condition—we all have a deep-seated need to share our moments of joy with others, just as when we experience the most horrific of calamities. Cautiously I looked at Süleyman and said, "Do you see now? Our boys trounced the enemy."

He smiled at me with uncomprehending eyes.

*

And that's how winter passed, a remarkable winter. Because I was always on the battlefront in heart and soul, I escaped the monotony of the season relatively unscathed.

Day by day rumors that the Anatolian army was going to come under a full frontal attack gathered steam, and almost all of the dailies made mention of the impending conflict. The fact that the Istanbul government sent a delegation to Ankara proved that the national resistance movement was growing in strength. Why else would they visit the new capital? What did those officials want to say? Of course, they would recommend that Ankara take a stance of restraint and deference. They made me think of priests visiting a man on the gallows to offer a few words of consolation.

"Be brave, my son. Soon enough you'll move on to the next life. Eternal life. So tell me, what is your last wish?"

"To go on living!"

The priests wince and murmur, "Of course *we* get stuck with one of those plucky convicts."

Ankara says one thing, the Istanbul government says something entirely different. If the country wasn't immersed so deeply in tragedy, one might be tempted to laugh at the absurdity of the situation.

But barefoot, bare-chested villagers are driving before them oxcarts creaking under the weight of bullets and cannonballs . . .

What's under that tattered dirty blanket? A gun carriage. What are those men doing in that trench over there? Skinning the carcass of an ox. Why? So they can make sandals for the soldiers.

As for our enemies, they are wearing sturdy English boots as they march toward us, and their cannons are transported like effigies of gods in the back of Berliet trucks under crisp canvas tarps.

Because of everything I've seen, however, we should believe that we will be victorious. Our soldiers are wearing sandals made from the hides of oxen. Their gun carriages are wrapped in blankets they pulled from their own beds. I've heard that in Eskişehir they are melting down train rails so they can make breechblocks for their artillery. The other day I saw at a nearby station how they are running their trains without coal; as soon as a train stops, all of the passengers disembark and fan out, collecting all the wood they can find, and they load their haul onto the locomotive.

*

Locomotives, railways, stations . . . I forgot to write about those details, even though they were among the most important issues of the season for me. If you've ever spent an extensive period of time in a distant region of the Anatolian plains, you'll understand what it means to feast your eyes upon a means of transport that can whisk you off to a civilized city and the significance of coming across a line of telegraph poles. If you've no such experience, it's difficult to explain.

I should note, however, that I'm not writing with the aim of explaining anything to anyone. That notion has never crossed my mind, as I write for the sole purpose of conversing with myself. If one day this country is liberated from its oppressors and I return to my previous life, I will burn these pages out of fear that they could fall into someone else's hands.

In such a scenario, my protracted exile in this village would be stripped of all meaning, as it would be seized upon as a work of literature.

I enjoy the literary and artistic endeavors of others, but I refrain from engaging in them myself. The world of art and literature is populated solely by geniuses, behind whom trail a procession of pathetic impersonators and masqueraders.

*

I, however, am no masquerader. It's patently obvious to me I'm nothing but a naive, overgrown child, and I cannot seem to escape my own character. Although fate has subjected me to countless cases of injustice, disappointment, and deception, they have failed to mature me. To this day I'm still moved by a sense of child-like joy and pleasant daydreams, and guileless upwellings swell my heart.

For the last three mornings I've been stirred awake by excitement because there's a young coal-black donkey tethered in my stable. But that's nothing new to me; all the suffering I've endured in my life has done nothing to dampen the enthusiasm of my youth. As a child, I'd feel as though the balmy waves of an infinite, luminous sea were rushing through me whenever I thought about a new toy I'd received, regardless of what I was doing at the time, even while studying or just walking down the street. As the saying goes, I'd feel like I was walking on air. Everyone and everything around me were nothing less than a charming symbol of the essence of a beautiful, magical world which I'd only recently discovered.

In my eyes, all was animated by the same magic and imbued with the same quintessence; even my school, if that's where I was, and my teacher, if I was seated before him; even the narrow, damp, serpentine street I was tired of trudging up and down twice a day; even the courtyard of our mansion, which was as dank as a cellar in the winter and filled with sunlight in the summer like a broad expanse of desert. I was always filled with a desire to not only embrace and kiss the people I met, but also the objects I chanced upon. If you were to analyze the source of the wondrous gaiety that filled my young heart, what would you find? A wooden horse, a locomotive made from a painted tin can, or a small drum, the skin of which was doomed to burst in a few days . . . The implication is clear. The simplest of things—a piece of wood, a can—sufficed to infuse my child's spirit with a feeling of profound, infinite joy.

And here in this cauldron of hardship and misery, amid the ruins of the thirty-three years of my existence which has been rocked by all manner of calamities, that coal-black foal, that living toy if you will, fills me with the same happiness I felt in my youth, which means that the spirit inhabiting this ravaged body is one and the same.

On the battlefield, I've seen the roughest, most war-hardened soldiers tremble like frightened children when the final moment draws near, and as they fall to the ground, they cry out for their mothers in a voice as shrill as a young boy's. When I was in the grips of malarial convulsions, I too called out for my mother as they anaesthetized me with chloroform so they could amputate my arm, and for a fleeting moment I saw her leaning toward me, a look of deep concern in her eyes as she stroked my hair.

I'm not sure why I thought of her. Pallid ghost, why have you come? It is impossible for you to walk across this gravelly ground. You cannot place your hand on this rough-hewn door, nor can you sit on this wooden bedstead, which is harder than stone. This place reeks of filth and disinfectant. The blackened mounds you see in the stove came from a dunghill, a word you've probably only heard in proverbs. I cannot bear, my dear pale mother, to have you here even for a second—you were always so clean and tidy, scented with soap.

If Emine refused İsmail's advances and became mine, the first thing I'd do is give her a thorough scrubbing and then I'd burn that rustic attire of hers, the thick layers of which conceal the curves of her body. Why, so that I could transform her into a fashionable Istanbul girl? No, far from it . . . She'd get her glossy red hair done up in two thick braids that hang down her back. I'd buy her loose-sleeve blouses of raw silk, which she'd wear with the collar unbuttoned, and snug-ankle şalvar that she'd cinch around her waist with a sash tied in a large knot, leaving its embroidered ends to dangle free like our grand-mothers do. Although speaking would be out of the question except when absolutely necessary, I'd tolerate giggles during moments of delight and occasional squeals when she was seized by paroxysms of astonishment, anger, or stubbornness, or if she was dabbling in the wiles of the coquette. In addition, I'd expect her to cook for and look after me.

While I was eating, having coffee, or working, I'd ask her to stand at the ready in case I needed anything. I'd never indulge her with petting and kissing à la the European mode of romance, but I would derive a certain pleasure from amusing myself with her as if she were a Van cat. In fact, how is she different, if at all, from the cats particular to the region of Van? Is she not majestic and elegant like them, and just as natural in her instincts? Could she also not be aptly described as a living, breathing embellishment of nature? My Emine is no cleverer than a Van cat, so is there truly any difference between her manner of speaking and the mewing of kittens?

That line of thought suddenly seemed so reasonable, so simple to realize, that I set off at once. The warm spring air scented with the fresh grass of the meadows buoyed my hopes and gave me courage. My dream became a little more real with each step I took, and as I walked, I murmured to myself, "I'm going to go straight to her aunt's house. In the clearest and firmest of terms, I'll say, 'I have money but I'm all alone in the world. Thanks to my savings, I don't need to work for a living. I saw Emine and I've taken a liking to her. Give her to me in marriage, and I'll make sure your needs are met for the rest of your life.'" I assumed she'd be surprised, unable to believe her ears at first, most likely surmising that I was lying or toying with her to entertain myself. But I'd maintain the most solemn composure. I'd say, "As you can see, I only have one arm. I need a companion who can take good care of me. When I was living with Zeynep Kadın, her girls and daughter-in-law looked after my needs, cooking my meals and washing my laundry. But now I live alone. For the time being, a man by the name of Süleyman is my caretaker, but the poor wretch is half-mad."

At that point, Emine's aunt would probably think I was out of my mind and say to herself, *He's got money, so why'd he decide to live alone here like an unwanted stranger? Why'd he leave Istanbul, only to endure a life of suffering in exile?* The look in her eyes would betray her suspicions. In an attempt to win her over, I'd tell her the mournful tale of my misadventures.

But with her provincial, realistic logic toughened by years of living in a village, would she be able to grasp the significance of the misfortunes I've endured? Would the anguish that drove me to these barren plains not seem pointless and childish to her? How could I convince her of the gravity of my situation?

By the time I arrived in Emine's village, my courage was faltering and I'd lost the steadfastness of purpose that had guided me there.

And when people started glancing at me strangely as I walked down the street, my resolve crumpled altogether. Naturally, I put on an air of aloofness and strolled around for some time, but when I reached the other side of the village, I fled into the fields.

*

However, the idea of taking Emine for myself lingered in my mind. When I was at home alone, it seemed like the most practical and sensible course of action, especially when I was lying in bed at night. But whenever I stepped outside, determined to make my dreams a reality, I'd be stopped in my tracks by the outlandishness of such an endeavor, as it would suddenly strike me as being not only foolish and laughable, but also highly unusual given the circumstances.

In the end, I decided that consulting a friend was my best option. By doing so, I'd perhaps be able to get some advice and we could work together to achieve my goal. The only problem was that I had no one in my life. To whom could I open up? Süleyman? Zeynep Kadın? Bekir Çavuş?

Bekir Çavuş . . . Why not? Prompted by that "Why not?" I began spending more time with him, waiting for an opportune moment to broach the subject. When we were alone, I'd ramble for hours, incapable, however, of getting to the point. I felt as bashful and awkward as a child attending a new school for the first time.

Then one day it happened. I'm not sure if he was being more garrulous than usual or if I got the impression he was in a sympathetic mood, but I said to him, "This loneliness is tearing at me. More than anything, people need a companion in life. Especially nobodies like me. We need someone who can look after us."

Bekir Çavuş failed to grasp what I was driving at. "Doesn't

Süleyman help you out?"

"Süleyman . . . Come on, that's not that I'm talking about. I need a woman."

At last it sunk in. "Well sir," he said, "get married. Don't you know some people in Istanbul? Write a letter and ask them to find someone for you."

"Do you think an Istanbul girl would come to this place? Even if she did, I wouldn't want her. Istanbul girls are too coy, too delicate. I need a strong young woman who can take care of me. I wouldn't even mind marrying a village girl from around here."

Bekir Çavuş shot me a look of surprise tinged with suspicion.

"I mean it," I said. "Take, for example, that orphan girl Emine who lives in [X] village. I'd marry her if she'd have me."

"Which Emine?"

"Maybe you've heard of her. İsmail wants to take her as his wife. But if they haven't gotten engaged yet . . ."

"Ah, yes. I knew her father. A good man. But I don't know much about Emine. He was in the army with me. Got killed during the war, but I don't know where."

And then the conversation started drifting as he blathered about the time he'd spent in Damascus, Crete, and Shkodra, which meant I'd have to wait for another day to catch Bekir Çavuş in the right mood and raise the issue yet again . . .

In the meantime, I kept finding myself walking down the road to Emine's village. I'd spend hours in the copse of poplar trees, hoping for an opportunity to speak with her about my intentions, but not once did I see her as I knelt by the stream, keeping a close watch on the pathway. One time, however, I came across İsmail during my idle wanderings, and while I decided to ignore him, the shameless runt sidled up to me. And what was troubling him? He wanted some cigarettes.

*

I eventually managed to explain my plans to Bekir Çavuş. He thought for a while and said, "If anyone can set it up, my woman can. I'll talk to her."

Two days later, I asked, "So what happened?"

"Ah," he sighed, grinning. "It slipped my mind. Tonight I'll bring it up, God willing."

Finally one day he came to me and said, "It's done. She's going to talk to the girl."

And thus began a period of great excitement in my life. At the same time, however, I found myself plagued by regrets, because if word got out about my intentions, I'd be in a difficult situation with Mehmet Ali's family. How would Zeynep Kadın feel about me? And what of İsmail, whom I loathed so much? Would he not leap at the opportunity to scorn me? Worst of all, I'd be unable to defend what I'd done, and I'd be forced to admit to myself that I'd behaved in a rather ignoble manner.

I wished I'd never spoken with Zeynep Kadın or İsmail about Emine. If I'd made advances to the girl without knowing he wanted to marry her, everything would've been different. But it was too late. The disgrace was done and I'd be doomed to hang my head in shame, even before the likes of little İsmail.

And as if that prospect wasn't horrific enough, what if she turned me down? I chided myself for having slipped into such a predicament. Hoping to redeem myself, I decided to call it off.

"Bekir Çavuş, tell your wife not to trouble herself over this trivial matter."

He looked down. Lost in thought, he stood there for a while, and then with the back of his hand he started slowly stroking his beard, which was as sparse and wiry as the whiskers of a cat. At first, I thought he was angry with me because I'd changed my mind.

"I thought long and hard about this, and in the end I decided it isn't in my best interests. And there's the matter of İsmail, who already said he wants to marry her. There would be bad blood between us."

"Well," he said, speaking with slow deliberation, "that girl's no good for you anyway. My wife went to talk to her. 'I won't marry a stranger,' she said. These village girls are odd. The whole lot of them's afraid of strangers. They're born and grow up here. Never see anything else. All of them are ignorant, completely ignorant. When I was in Crete . . ."

I can't recall what Bekir Çavuş said after that point, but I'm fairly certain my lips curled into a warped smile and I could feel the skin of my face growing tight. A wave of self-pity was building up inside me. I wasn't sure if I was going to break down in tears or burst out laughing.

In my state of bewilderment, I kept holding out my cigarette case to Bekir Çavuş, and without a moment of hesitation he took a cigarette every time. When I finally came to my senses and looked up, he looked like an automatic tabletop cigarette dispenser that had gone haywire, as he had cigarettes tucked behind his ears, clutched in his palm, and wedged between his fingers.

The normal reaction in such a situation would be to double over in laughter, but my jaw was clenched tight. Getting to my feet, I staggered off. I'm not even sure if I said goodbye.

The tops of the hills were glowing in the last light of day and the hooves of the livestock were pounding the dry ground as they returned to their stables. It was dark in my home when I stepped inside. Not bothering to light a lamp, I lay down on the divan. I felt as though I'd fallen into a briar patch, as every inch of my skin was stinging. I had no idea what I should do.

Is this the kind of moment, I thought, *when one commits suicide? Could life get any worse?*

Normally I enjoy suffering. There was nothing pleasant about the torment I felt that day, however, because it was not the result of a large-scale disaster. What I was experiencing was the anguish of a man who has been humiliated, and that feeling of shame clings to you like a bat sucking blood from a gash in the middle of your forehead. Drained of strength, your body goes as limp as a carcass. Something base and repugnant happens deep down inside you, which is why being ashamed is analogous to loathing oneself.

If we don't succumb to the allure of suicide at such times, when should we? What difference does it make anyway, since we're already fetid with the stench of rotting flesh? Our sole haven is underground. Only burial can purify us. But does the earth really have the power to purify?

Why did I think of that? When I was a child, I heard an old woman say something similar. Her daughter had run off with a sergeant who was serving in a regiment under my father's command. Sprawled on the ground in front of my mother, the old woman was wailing, "Now only the earth can purify her body!"

At the time, I didn't understand what she meant, but now, twenty-five years later, her words resonate with profound meaning. All the same, an image of her face keeps appearing in my mind, making me laugh. My chuckles, however, sound odd in my ears, like the sob-choked laughter of the duped fool in the opera *Pagliacci*.

I can't bring myself to leave my room. When I get out of bed, I only make it as far as my divan, where I lie down again. From there, I eventually make my way back to the bedstead, because I lack the strength to do anything else. I'm like a wind-up toy whose springs are broken.

Everything wearies me. The slightest of sounds grate on my ears. The light of day is too much to bear. When Süleyman sits by my bedside, his breathing becomes so intolerable that I want to drive him out of my house.

"What is it now?" I snap. "Why are you sitting there, gawking at me?"

"Don't you have any work to do? Why do you just sit there all the time?"

"Leave me alone. I don't want anything. Not water, not food. Nothing. Go away."

Those are the kinds of things I say to Süleyman when I open my mouth to speak. Since the poor man has never seen me in my darker states of despair, he's so baffled that his few remaining shreds of intellect have fluttered away.

*

One morning I awoke to find that Süleyman was gone. I waited, expecting him to show up by evening. But he didn't. When two days passed and he still hadn't come around, I decided to go out in search of him. Under the cover of night, I walked as far as his house. He wasn't there. While I was plodding back home, I ran into Memiş as he was slipping as silently as a ghost along one of the village walls.

"Memiş, have you seen Süleyman?"

It took him a few minutes to recognize me and just as long to comprehend what I was saying.

Eventually Memiş said gravely, "He's at the old mosque."

I walked to the mosque, which was dark, and Memiş trailed behind me. I called out, "Süleyman . . . Süleyman, are you here?" When I didn't get a reply, I stepped through the doorway.

The old mosque was more or less abandoned when a new one was built by the village square near the fountain. Now it's only used on religious holidays, nights of the Tarawih prayers, and celebrations marking the birth of the Prophet Muhammed. At the same time, anyone can sleep there for the night, regardless of whether they're from the village or elsewhere.

I asked Memiş to light a match, whereupon I saw Süleyman curled up asleep on a straw mat at the far end of the mosque.

"Hey, Süleyman," I said. "What are you doing here?"

By the time he grunted in reply, the match had burned out. I walked toward him and, when Memiş lit another match, I saw that Süleyman was looking at me.

"Get up. I've come to take you back to my place."

Pouting, he mumbled, "Why? What do you want with me?"

I took a step closer to him.

"What kind of question is that? You left me all alone. My place is a mess."

I asked Memiş to light another match. As he sat there on the mat refusing to budge, Süleyman had the air of a Hindu guru. Seeing that my attempts to coax him like a child were failing, I said sternly, "Süleyman, on your feet now. This is going too far."

But he merely repeated, "What do you want with me?"

"Very well," I said. "If you don't want to come back, I'll hire some-one else." And I strode away.

As of tonight, I'm completely alone. I'll have to manage everything with my one arm, including cooking my meals and sweeping my house. If I can't find a woman in the village to wash my laundry, by force of circumstance I'm going to do it myself. I'm a modern-day Robinson Crusoe surrounded by the endless, barren plains of Anatolia, and my house is no different than a desolate island far out at sea.

Will a ship rescue me one day? If so, I can only hope its name is the *Anatolian Brigade*. Every hour of every day I sit staring out my window, which is like a crenel in the wall of a castle. The horizon is disturbingly calm and still. Something isn't right—aren't we in the midst of a war? I feel as though the apprehensions stirred up by my imagination are shaping the world around me, and the sporadic reports I read in the newspapers do nothing to settle my rattled nerves. The agony of waiting can be felt on all fronts. Political efforts to secure peace have failed, and the delegation sent to London came back empty-handed. As always, Europe maintains its position as a deaf wall in its relations with us.

Despite everything, when the forlorn inhabitant of this desolate island peers out of his cave, he sees a port's green and red lanterns. Those lights are a symbol of my hope. Where does the oil come from? Who trims and lights the wicks? I don't know, but that hope is my only sustenance, the final glimmer of my will to live. And if it goes out . . .

I can't even imagine what will happen.

*

Loneliness is an ache that never abates.

If someone attempts to glorify isolation as salvation of the self, you can be certain they have fallen into error. When human beings— which are herd animals by nature—hold to ideas that run contrary to those of others, they are destined to live out their lives as miserable creatures drifting from place to place. Their only hope for consolation is to return to the herd.

But what of my flock? Where is our shepherd? Perched atop the rugged boulders in Ankara, he is calling out, trying to bring us together. Greetings, great shepherd! May your war be blessed! But when at last you do gather your herd, will I be summoned as well? Will this village be counted among its ranks? Most likely not. What does the shepherd have to say? This village is moldering away by itself on these plains, and I will go on choking back my tears in solitude. There will be no conciliation between us.

The conflagration engulfing the world failed to bring us together, and the Day of Judgment couldn't heal the rift between us.

In the early days of the armistice, an acquaintance said to me, "I'm afraid of neither their tanks nor their troops, and the machine guns they've placed on nearly every street don't scare me either. What *does* frighten me, however, is the discord among us Turks. That is what's going to destroy us in the end." At the time, I thought to myself, *He's basing his argument on the state of affairs in Istanbul, ascribing the confusion and turmoil that is rampant among its citizens to the rest of the country without accounting for that fact that the true motherland lies in Anatolia, which has been untainted by the strife and filth of the city. Those lands have become sacred, kneaded for years with a yeast of life that has simmered over the stark flames of anguish.*

I believed that there were sincere, pure-hearted, impassioned people in this country. I believed that the rich would fling open their doors to the poor and that the countless paths of exile would lead to homes with warm hearths. In my eyes, all the women of Anatolia were mothers and all the children were joined in sisterhood and brotherhood. The stones were our companions, and while it was well known that poverty was widespread, I thought I'd find a spiritual wealth buried deep within.

And what do I see now? Anatolia, a land of muftis advising the enemy, village leaders showing the way for our foes, town notables banding with plunderers to loot their neighbors' lands, adulterous women opening their bosoms to deserters, false Sufis with faces ravaged by syphilis, religious fanatics chasing young boys in the courtyards of mosques . . .

So many young men filled with fresh ideas and hope, their heads crushed under stones because they dared trim their mustaches with scissors. So many soldiers facing down the enemy, only to be shot in the back by the people for whom they were fighting. The path of our leader and symbol of independence has been cut off time and time again, and his city has been besieged equally often. I, Ahmet Celâl, madman of the motherland, lunatic citizen, crippled casualty of war, am utterly alone in this place.

And once again you are at fault, enlightened Turks! What have you done for this broken nation and its impoverished masses? For years, even centuries, you sucked the people dry of blood and tossed their remains onto the arid ground, and yet you still feel you have every right to be repulsed by them.

The people of Anatolia have souls, but you failed to guide them. They have minds, but you failed to educate them. They have bodies, but you failed to feed them. They have the land on which they live. Even so, you failed to cultivate it. You left them to their animal instincts and ignorance, though they were under the constant threat of famine. Between the hard earth and parched sky, they grew like weeds. And now you come with your scythes. But when you've sown nothing, what will you reap? These nettles and brown thistles? Of course they'll prick your feet and tear into your skin—what did you expect? As blood flows from your innumerable wounds, you grimace in pain. Out of anger you ball your hands into fists. But know that your suffering is the consequence of your own handiwork.

*

The days drag on, while the months fly past! Yet again summer is here. But summer of which year? Let's see what the newspapers say . . . They are stacked like small pyramids in the other room. If they were to topple down on me, I'd suffocate under their weight.

And how dusty they've become! On some days, I feel like I can't breathe. I'd like nothing more than to have those newspapers tossed into the village bakery's furnace, but Emeti Kadın refuses to even touch them because of the portraits piled on top of the stacks (when Süleyman stopped coming around, I hired on an old woman named Emeti to look after me, which she does in the most cursory manner). Although she's been in my employ for several months now, she hasn't dared take a step into that room for fear that the "spirits" in my collection of drawings, paintings, and figurines will bring her harm. Emeti Kadın looks upon me with fear and wonder, as well as a certain amount of apprehension, because I live among such items. In the early days of her employment with me, she came face to face with a bust of Socrates that was on top of my wardrobe.

"Don't that thing scare you at night?" she asked.

Emeti Kadın is as stout as the stump of an oak tree. Her face is so pockmarked that, when viewed from the front, it resembles the heart of a head of cauliflower. Add a slathering of grime, as if the head of cauliflower had been freshly torn from the earth during a storm, and the image is complete.

One day I asked, "Emeti Kadın, don't you ever wash your face?"

"I got no time for that," she said. "Before the sun comes up, I gotta get things ready for the boy and pack up some food for him, and then I gotta get the cow ready for milking. When that's done, I fire up the stove to boil the milk, and then I come running here. You're single, you don't have any cows or goats, but there's lots of work. Like you tell me to heat up some tea . . . Wash the dishes from yesterday in hot water . . . Every day you want me to cook food. You see how the days go with you? When I get home at night the boy's hungry and tired. I boil up milk for him, put in some bread. Sometimes he wants cheese and onions, other times he tells me to make some gruel."

The "boy" is Emeti Kadın's grandson Hasan, whom she looks after by herself. He tends to their herd.

Despite the fact that he's only around eleven or twelve years old, he understands the gravity of his work and responsibilities, which he undertakes with great solemnity.

It saddens me that I hadn't met him sooner. I had, however, seen him returning to the village as he guided the herd down the slopes of distant hills on some evenings. At the time, I only saw him as an allegory of sorts. One of the sons of Jacob . . . I hadn't felt a need to distinguish him from the other young shepherds mentioned in the account of the lives of the prophets known as the *Kısas-ı Enbiya*. But when I got to know him, I immediately realized he was a young man of singular character.

Like İsmail, he never laughs. In fact, he's so somber that I feel like a frivolous, spoiled child when I'm around him. A few times I tried to engage him in light banter but failed miserably, which left me in a glum state of mind.

On his scrawny shoulders, which are always clad in threadbare, patched shirts, he bears the nobility of an affluent man who's fallen on hard times, inspiring in others a feeling of respect as well as deep sadness. I wonder if perhaps, generations back, his forefathers had once been men of the city.

While İsmail is similarly quiet and staid, his graveness is the direct result of a physical rather than a spiritual affliction. Graced with eyes as dazzling as those of a gazelle, Hasan stands apart as a god in his beauty. The delicate lines of his high, narrow cheeks and his graceful lips seem to be a hidden reflection of the refinement that the Flemish painters were so fond of depicting in their portraits.

In contrast, İsmail's sunken mouth . . .

Still, what kind of comparison can be drawn between a wizened dwarf and a tender youth?

Ever since he became a nightmare haunting my life, I've found no respite from İsmail, neither in thought nor feeling, particularly after he married Emine and brought her to the village . . .

Ah, I forgot to record in these pages the fact that they were wed.

*

How did it happen? I'm still dumbfounded. What drove Zeynep Kadın to give her consent? How did İsmail get his way in the end? There's only one explanation: Since there was no wedding or ceremony, it must've been a fait accompli.

I found out by coincidence. One day Bekir Çavuş and I were on our way to look at a plot of land I wanted to buy. As we passed Mehmet Ali's place, whom did I see but Emine and her new sister-in-law standing in front of the door. I glanced at Bekir Çavuş, who said, "Well, your guy went off and married the girl."

We walked on for a hundred, maybe a hundred and fifty paces. Or maybe we didn't walk that far at all. I stopped.

"It's rather hot today," I said. "Why don't we wait for another day?"

"Fine with me," he replied.

We turned around, taking the path that runs behind the village.

All night long I kept asking myself, "What was I thinking?" I was incapable, however, of answering that question definitively. I think she giggled when she saw me. But was it disdainful laughter? Or the kind prompted by an unexpected encounter with an acquaintance?

I then decided that she hadn't actually laughed. Instead, she'd angrily looked away, covering her mouth with her headscarf. No, that wasn't right either. Rather, those green eyes framed by her olive-skinned face were as aloof and oblivious as two damp leaves that had fallen to the ground. I didn't even see a flash of recognition in her expression, meaning that perhaps she hadn't actually seen me. Maybe she'd been distracted by something when we walked by. In any case, she would've seen my left side, not my right. Only if she'd seen the empty sleeve swinging from my shoulder would she have definitively recognized me.

During the course of our acquaintanceship, which had lasted more than a year, not once had she looked me in the face, nor had our eyes ever made contact . . . How had she described me to İsmail? "That guy missing an arm." In her view, that was my one distinguishing feature: A nonexistent arm.

What a cruel creature! Hadn't she heard the trembling in my voice whenever I spoke to her? Hadn't she felt my compassionate gaze brush against her skin like gentle fingertips? On that day when I knelt down beside her, hadn't she noticed the pounding of my heart? Or had I passed through her life without leaving even the slightest impression on her heart and mind?

If I had, then surely I would've sensed something when I saw her today. Indeed, it would've been inevitable.

But what does it matter? The spell was broken when I discovered she'd married İsmail. His puckered mug pressed against the fresh skin of her face . . . That is inseparable from Emine now. Isn't imagining the two of them snuggled up in bed reason enough to be repulsed by her? Unhappily for me, however, repulsion does not involve the release of forgetting.

Delving deep into our imaginations, we fashion effigies of the ideal woman which we purify to gem-like perfection in the flames of our passion, only to be double-stricken by sorrow when they run off with the most brutish of beasts or let themselves slip into mud-thick bogs, as we feel the grief of the scorned creator as well as the pain of losing a most prized possession.

Our inner voice laments, "What's done is done and there's no turning back," which means that even if she were to return, we wouldn't take her because in our eyes she's defiled beyond redemption and reeks of irrevocable decay.

Chevalier de Grieux took the cold body of Manon Lescaut into his arms and kissed her. In contrast, Dostoyevsky's guileless protagonist couldn't bear being in the presence of his dead lover's fetid corpse. Still, the stench didn't drive the longing from his heart and though he tried to flee from his feelings, he was caught firmly in their grasp.

*

"Hasan, how can you call yourself a shepherd when you don't have a pan flute?"

He blinked at me in confusion because he didn't know the meaning of "pan flute." I'd come across him one evening on the slopes of the mountain. He was leaning on his shepherd's crook as he watched his herd grazing in a meadow down below, just like the herdsmen Virgil described in his poems. Those idyllic shepherds were probably just as plain and modest, embodied by certain glances and movements.

"Hasan, what do you do all day by yourself? Don't you get bored?"

In lieu of a reply he squatted down. I could tell by his expression that the notion of tedium was completely alien to him. How delectable to be spared such angst! As I see it, Hasan is a wondrous being.

Kneeling down beside him, I said, "I suppose being out here all alone doesn't frighten you."

Gazing at me with his glistening dark eyes, he replied, "People say there're wolves out here, but I never seen them. Late one night I heard some howling, but pretty far away. A chill went down my spine. I set out going back home. Whenever the sheep hear a wolf, they run quick for the village."

"How about your dogs? Are they fierce?"

"One of them's as fierce as three wolves. The other day two guys came up to me. Said they wanted a few sheep. When I said no, they got aggressive but the dogs laid into them, and they ran off."

I listened to Hasan with the rapt attention of a child. As he sensed we were becoming closer, he opened up more to me.

"They can smell anything, even a thousand paces away. One day out behind Koçaş village the dogs sniffed out a dead man in a creek. I went and told the villagers about it. But no one knew who he was. His body was all black and swelled up tight as a drum. 'Must be a stranger,' they said. They buried him so he wouldn't stink. You think we should've told the gendarmes?"

"Of course."

"But they got so much on their hands these days. All kinds of riff-raff going around. Just yesterday I saw three deserters."

"Did they see you?"

"They asked me for some bread. When I gave them a loaf, they said, 'Don't tell anyone you saw us. If you do, we'll come back and smash your head in.' You're the first person I told about this. Don't say a word to anyone."

A weighty silence settled over us. I felt as aggrieved as a commanding officer who'd lost a pitched battle, and he was as motionless as a statue carved from stone.

"Deserters," I said. "That's bad. Worse even than death."

Hasan hung his head as if he himself had run off from the army.

Hearing about deserters, especially these days when the enemy is preparing to launch an offensive, makes me sick in spirit and soul. What of the front that fell in the War of '93 and the constant defeats we've suffered since? This place marks the frontier of the homeland.

Is this not our last line of defense? What room for retreat is left to us?

*

As I write these lines, I think the enemy is moving into position for its assault. For me, the entire summer was spent in infernal, solitary waiting.

While everyone else was busy ploughing, planting, and harvesting, I was hedged in by towering stacks of newspapers, wondering how that protracted tragedy would finally unfold. While everyone was talking, I fell silent. While everyone was looking after their herds, henhouses, and fields, I was listening to the thundering footsteps of the god of iron spewing fire into the sky on distant horizons.

The god of iron draws near. Is this a premonition? Mere conjecture, perhaps?

Not in the least. I based my conclusions on an official communiqué. For forty-eight hours I've been examining the labyrinthine and ambiguous text page by page in the same manner that seers would interpret Sibylline scrolls and Chaldean astrologers would translate the movement of heavenly bodies into prophecies. At long last, I succeeded in extricating the meaning that lurked beneath the surface: "It has been observed that the enemy is mobilizing the entirety of its troops through Uşak and Afyon."

Why weren't they marching along the Bursa-İnönü route? Why the change of direction?

I've been trying to understand the logic behind that maneuver by charting the movements of the enemy's forces. However, the tangled, web-like lines of their path overlaying the chaos of colors, shading, and place names on the map left me even more baffled.

Could it be a shortcut to Eskişehir? Maybe the road is more passable? After noting down the mountains along the route, I used a matchstick to measure the distances.

But my efforts yielded nothing of significance.

My imagination charged to the fore at the point where my data, knowledge, and calculations failed to provide satisfactory answers. By drawing on the speculative reports published in the Istanbul papers, I concluded that the enemy is going to make its final move in the upcoming battle. They were moving their king into position. Rumor has it that Prince Andrew is personally leading a battalion that has committed the most outrageous atrocities in the war.

I pray to God I'll be there for the day when we drive them into the sea in a glorious, merciless counterattack.

And why shouldn't I? My intuition tells me that victory will be ours.

If we are triumphant, I'll set out at once on the road to Izmir. Tirelessly I'll walk onward like the lovelorn men in ancient Turkish tales who wore iron sandals as they travelled far and wide in pursuit of their beloveds. At night, I'll sleep under the stars and gnaw on dry crusts of bread and march on during the day. Shunning villages and crowds, I'll press on toward the crisp blue waters of the gulf, clad in the crystalline armor of my rejoicing and dreams. And when I reach Izmir, I'll lie on the shore for hours, breathing in the scent of the sea-moist earth.

As I think of that impassioned journey, my entire being fills with bliss. The blood in my veins pulses afresh, my heart races with exhilaration, and I can feel the cool breeze of a spring night stroking my cheeks. I start singing to myself, which sends my excitement soaring to new peaks.

Sometimes during such moments of joy, I tease Emeti Kadın.

"I must say, you're looking young and spry today. What's your secret?"

"If you knew how this poverty and loneliness ruined me . . . I'd feel half my age if not for that. Hasan's father was killed in the war. My daughter, she died giving birth. The very same day that husband of hers threw us out on the street. What else could happen to poor old me? I been through it all."

"Throw off such gloomy thoughts. How about if I find you a nice man? Would you marry him?"

As bashful as a young girl, Emeti Kadın bows her head, a smile on her lips.

"Now, that's in fate's hands! But who'd want me?"

At times like that, I can tell she craves encouragement.

"Emeti Kadın, if we drive our enemy into the sea, I swear I'll do whatever it takes to get you married."

"Even if so, it's up to fate . . ."

"Why do you say that? As we speak, there's a war going on in Uşak and Afyon. When we drive the enemy back, we'll rally our troops in Izmir."

"Where's this Izmir place?"

"That's where we'll fight to the bitter end. After Istanbul, it's the biggest, richest city in the country . . ."

"Even bigger than Sivrihisar?"

Only once in her life had Emeti Kadın seen a city—and Sivrihisar at that!

"Emeti Kadın, Sivrihisar and Izmir couldn't be more different. For one, Izmir is on the sea. The houses, which are made of cut stone and marble, have huge iron gates. Everywhere you look there are vineyards, gardens, and groves of lemon and orange trees. Twenty Sivrihisars would fit in Izmir."

Judging by her expression, I got the feeling she placed little stock in what, for her, may have seemed a bizarre if not tall tale about an imaginary place, and since she appeared more interested in hearing about the prospects of marriage, I added, "As I was saying, when we win the war, I'll take you there myself and personally arrange the wedding."

She recoiled at the notion of leaving. "God forbid I leave my hometown! I was born here and I'll die here. You left your home, and look at you now!"

"Emeti Kadın, the enemy occupied my city. I had no choice but to leave."

My heart sank as I spoke those words. Getting up, I trudged back to my room, thinking, *If only I could be saved from this place. If only . . .*

How fortunate are the people who, day by day, even hour by hour, are kept abreast of the great battle raging on the frontlines in Uşak by a steady rain of telegrams and dispatches that soothe their hearts.

In critical times, bad news is better than no news. Every so often I get the urge to walk all the way to Eskişehir so I can learn first-hand how the conflict is proceeding. Once in a while I climb a distant hill and prick up my ears in the hope of hearing the booming of cannons—which would be impossible, of course, as the war is being fought over a hundred miles away.

It would be an untruth, however, to say that the issue is enshrouded in absolute silence. Everyone in the village comes up with their own version of events, which they voice without reservation, and these rumors take to the skies like invisible flocks of birds that fill the air with caws and chirps. Some of them are fantastical in nature, akin to the Phoenix. Who is setting them aflight? Whence do they take wing and where do they perch?

I don't know. Neither do those who understand their language. But to my astonishment, I've found that these rumors are almost always the same, regardless of the village in which they settle or who is spreading them. It's as though a radio station dedicated to promoting the propaganda of a certain political viewpoint is broadcasting a series of lies that follow a more or less standardized format.

According to these rumors, people are heading our way, but they aren't enemy troops. Rather, they're green-turbaned saints sent by a queen named Europe with the aim of saving us from the brigands roaming Anatolia. After rescuing us, the queen is going to convert to Islam, as commanded by her heart. Mustafa Kemal Pasha knows nothing about this turn of events because he is surrounded by objectionable men who are referred to as "culprits." These wicked figures have levied tithes and taxes across the entire country, which they pocket for their own gain. Our day of salvation, however, is upon us. The saints with green turbans use neither guns nor cannons, as they don't need them. All they do is recite a prayer and, with a single breath, a path is cleared before them.

As these stories were going around, who should show up in the village but Dervish Yusuf. The village was thrown into turmoil as hearts were set aflame in fits of ecstasy like the feverish convulsions brought on by swamp fever.

Emeti Kadın didn't come around to my place for two days. When she finally showed up, I asked, "Where have you been?"

"Around . . . I went to the dervish, had him read a prayer for me."

"What did he have to say? I mean, about the general state of the world?"

"I didn't ask. But others did."

"What did he say to them?"

"Same thing we always hear."

"Like what? That the enemy has overrun more than half the country and now they want to take all of Anatolia? That they've secured a position behind those mountains but we're heroically fighting back?"

"Mm, no . . . He said nothing like that."

And then Emeti Kadın launched into a lengthy explanation about the green-turbaned saints and the queen who longed to become Muslim.

My mind swirled with questions. Would she believe me if I told her it was all lies? How could I phrase it so she'd see the truth? Even if I could cross the chasm of centuries separating us, what could I say to actually change her mind? I knew that no matter how persistently I called out to her, she'd refuse to budge. Her way of thinking was lodged in the past, frozen hard as a rock. The words that fell from her lips were not her own. It was no different than reading, syllable by syllable, an inscription on an ancient tablet.

Still, I pressed on, pointing out that some of the men from the village, most notably Mehmet Ali, had gone to fight in the war.

"Why," I asked, "did they go? What are they doing? If those people you mentioned are coming to save us, why are the villagers taking up arms to fight and who are they fighting?"

Shaking her head, Emeti Kadın replied, "They're like me. How could they know?"

Aside from them, is there anyone in this country who truly knows what they're doing? War is the only reality now. For me, all those men who aren't on the frontlines are freaks of nature—above all, myself. In the same way that the sea drives corpses forward on waves choked with flotsam until they wash up on a remote beach, we've been stranded on the slopes of these barren hills. There is nothing in this place but putrid stagnancy, malarial tremors, and life's parasitic bursts of verdure, and not a single spark of the sacred fire setting the battlegrounds ablaze can be seen from here.

Once in a while I walk the road that leads to the Sarıköy train station, asking passersby if they have news about the war. Some people don't know anything, while others make statements that seem a far cry from reality. Yet others say things that are so bleak, vile, and repugnant that I don't want to believe them; when I walk home in the evening, I find that my thoughts are in utter disarray, and upon arriving, I can only bring myself to take a few bites of the food Emeti Kadın prepared for me. Half-hungry, I collapse on the bed, and my sleep is haunted by nightmares all through the night.

Sometimes when I'm asleep I hear voices speaking in Greek. Leaping out of bed, I rush to the open window and peer outside. My ears ring and sweat runs down my temples as I glance anxiously around.

On one such occasion, the moon was out, bathing the landscape in a wan, lifeless, suspicious glow. It occurred to me that night was nothing but the pale corpse of the day. Shuddering, I withdrew back into my room.

It was an insidious light, like the glimmer in the eyes of an enemy soldier ready to pounce on you at any moment. Indeed, the enemy creeps forward under the cover of that gloom.

Wait, what did I say? The enemy is moving forward? This can only mean one thing: I, too, have started believing in the sinister rumors going around. But was the voice I heard in my head really *my* voice? Were those words *my* words? No, absolutely not! I meant to say, "We're grappling with the enemy in that gloom." What I said was the result of fatigue, a mere slip of the tongue. How could the enemy draw near, when we all know that they won't make it this far?

On another night, I awoke with a start from an even more

harrowing dream in which a band of Evzone troops from the Greek army had encircled me. As they stood there with their long mustaches and tassels, I realized that I was being put on trial. I wanted to defend myself but my voice caught in my throat, producing a sound like the gurgling of a spigot when the water has been shut off, and the Evzones were becoming increasingly agitated. Suddenly they drew their pistols and took aim. As their fingers curled around the triggers of their guns, I woke up, my heart beating wildly in my chest.

On yet another night I had a dream that was so realistic I couldn't distinguish between my waking and sleeping states even long after I'd opened my eyes. In the dream, Bekir Çavuş and I were in the village square, which was thronged with people. Despite our efforts to remain side by side, the crowd kept pulling us apart, and finding one another again proved to be almost impossible. Under the dazzling light of the sun, I could clearly see the faces of all the people who were there. Some of them came from the village while others were complete strangers, and although they were speaking a variety of different languages, many of which I didn't know, strangely I was able to understand what everyone was saying.

They were eagerly awaiting the arrival of a dignitary, or perhaps a delegation. People kept anxiously glancing at their watches and some of the men had clambered up to higher ground so they could peer out at the road in the distance. All at once a woman came running down a village lane toward the crowd, screaming at the top of her voice.

The woman was Zeynep Kadın. It was so obviously her; never before had I seen her face in such minute detail, down to the last wrinkle and pockmark. Her teeth were knocking together and tears as large as chickpeas were rolling down her cheeks. As she ran, her headscarf slipped back, and strands of hennaed hair fell across her face.

Powerfully parting the crowd, I dashed toward her.

"Don't worry," I said. "I'm going to douse the flames." And then I started running as quickly as I could. Behind me, the crowd burst into laughter. A few times I spun around and bellowed, "Dogs! Scoundrels!"

I shouted so loudly that I woke myself up. When I drifted off to sleep again, by strange coincidence I slipped back into the same dream. Zeynep Kadın's house was enveloped in sooty flames. İsmail and Mehmet Ali's wife and sisters were trying to put out the fire with small cups of water.

My voice cracking with anger and concern, I was yelling, "How can you put out a fire like that? Don't you have any buckets or basins?"

"They're all in the house!"

I glanced around, hoping to catch sight of Emine.

"Where's Emine?"

They cried out, "Oh God, she's still inside!"

At once I dashed into the billowing smoke.

When I awoke from the nightmare, I was still looking for Emine, desperately peering into the darkness of my room, wondering if I'd see the body of a young woman in flames.

I struggled through the night, and for the rest of the next day I was weighed down with sorrow, feeling grieved by that tragedy.

Ominous dark clouds filled the sky from one end of the horizon to the other. But what need was there for that? Not a day goes by that three or four enemy airplanes don't fly overhead. One time they swooped so low that we could see the blue and white of their underwings. Another time they threw leaflets to the ground. I got ahold of one of them. It read: "We've secured control of Eskişehir and Kütahya. Very soon we'll be here as well. Do not abandon your homes. We will bring you no harm. The Sultan and Caliph are on our side. We're fighting to save you from Kemal's bandits."

When the villagers heard the message, their eyes lit up with joy.

Only Bekir Çavuş was concerned. Shaking his head, he said, "They may be saying things like that now, but don't believe a word of it. Soon enough they'll start taking everything they can get their hands on. Not a single loaf of bread, not even an egg, will be left in the village. Not even a stick of hay. And they'll make off with the oil, all the herds of goat and sheep. If you ask me, we should find a way to hide them now while there's still time."

Salih Ağa smirked and said, "Well, I happened to hear they pay for everything they take."

"Once, maybe twice. But how're they going to pay more? They're soldiers. They don't make a fortune in the places where they go."

But no one was listening to Bekir Çavuş, choosing instead to side with Salih Ağa.

"They're not coming to stay for good! A day or two later and they'll be on their way."

Bekir Çavuş replied, "There's a saying that goes, 'Soldiers don't plant crops on the march.' Sure they'll go, but they won't leave anything behind. Winter's coming, and we'll be left with nothing."

As I sat off to the side listening to that banal, despicable conversation taking place on the eve of a catastrophe of national scope, my heart was in my throat. I can no longer bring myself to say anything, and I wonder if it wouldn't be better for me to trek further inland. There certainly must be trains carrying the wounded from Eskişehir. I could board one of them and go to Ankara. At the very least, I'd be among people who grasp the meaning and essence of this tragedy.

No, no. I no longer have the strength for such an undertaking. I'll stay here and die here. On the day when the enemy enters the village, I'll put on my military uniform and face them swinging my sword so they can pierce my body again and again with their bayonets . . .

Even now I can feel the deep, divine pleasure derived from falling victim to acts of gory torment. The old accounts of martyrs say that when a soldier dies, his corpse riddled with hundreds of arrows, a rose blossoms from each of the wounds. Now I understand just how true that may be, for every single point on my body where I imagine they will plunge their bayonets now itches ever so sweetly that only a rose could bloom from the wound and honey trickle forth instead of blood.

The worst calamity of all, however, would be if the enemy troops simply pass through, leaving me unscathed, as in that case I would be little more than the ruins of a hovel, condemned to rot away in life.

As the villagers spoke, it was like listening to the murmurings of a gathering of creatures from a different world, beings of a different race. Sometimes I didn't understand what they were saying. Wheat, barley, herd, oxen, hay? What will those things mean?

*

For a few days it's been possible to observe how the front is falling. A murky flood of exodus began flowing down the roads passing by the districts of Haymana and Sivrihisar. Trudging among the refugees, who are mostly women, children, and the aged, there are demoralized troops as well. They are dead-eyed, and they look like they've lost all sense of humanity and been reduced to a most primitive state of being. That's why I don't try talking with them. I do, however, walk alongside some of the others, asking where they're coming from and where they're going. Most of them are from the region of Eskişehir, but some have come from as far away as Kütahya and Bilecik. Indeed, they know where they've come from but have no idea where they're going.

They are a motley lot. As they walk, some are carrying bedrolls on their shoulders, some have bundles under their arms, some have babies swaddled on their backs, and some have put pots on their heads like helmets. Like the current of the Porsuk River, their movement forward is unthinking, pointless, and woeful . . .

Sometimes I bring them parcels of food, which they take without thanking me and silently plod on.

One day I asked a white-bearded man whose expression still bore traces of humanity, "Is there no hope left?"

After looking me in the eye and gazing at my right side, he walked off without answering. The old man's behavior struck such misery into my heart that I couldn't bring myself to look at him as he trudged away. My head fell forward and I collapsed on my knees.

Another day I came across a boy ten or twelve years of age who'd lost his way on the barren plains. He was weeping as he walked. When he saw me, he screamed and raced off in the other direction. I yelled "Stop!" but he kept running, never once looking back. I chased after him but I couldn't catch up as he dashed across streams and over hills. In the end, he vanished. It was so hot I thought he'd evaporated into the air.

One time I came across an old woman who'd been abandoned on the side of the road like an old bundle. A wizened, dusky old woman . . . So tattered were her clothes that at first I thought she was a scarecrow that had fallen to the ground. She was lying there, curled up. Leaning over her, I asked, "Granny, are you sick?"

"Sick? What are you talking about? They wouldn't give me any food. They wouldn't give me anything to drink. For seven days and nights they made me walk. I told that worthless daughter of mine, 'Carry me a little.' That was what I did wrong. They said, 'You wait here for a little. We'll come get you.' Lies, lies, lies . . . I knew they was lying, but sir, what could I do?"

Her voice was so frail that it was like the buzzing of a mosquito.

She didn't have any teeth, so when her mouth was closed, her lower lip pressed against the bottom of her nose.

"Come with me to my village."

"No, I can't do that! Maybe they'll come back. They'll come back and won't be able to find me."

One night, a voice from the gloom commanded, "Don't move!"

But I continued walking. Then a bullet whizzed past my ear like a wasp and I heard the pounding of feet of someone running. The sound of boots with nails in the soles. Obviously it was a deserter.

I was nearly killed by a bullet from the gun of a Turkish private.

Indeed, the front lines had obviously collapsed.

But does that mean a complete collapse? No, the Turkish army hasn't fallen apart. A voice rings out over Ankara, proclaiming, "The enemy might advance, even as far as Ankara. But we're going to defend ourselves from atop the last boulder of our homeland. We're going to strangle the enemy in the sanctuary of the nation." That is His voice. A voice that gives people hope, strength, and resolve.

The Grand National Assembly convened with new determination, appointing Him as the Commander in Chief with broad powers. He personally is coming to the battlefield . . . Goldenhead has started gleaming on the horizon like Venus.

The herd of rams that seemed to be scattering is now pulling back together. I've seen military convoys heading to new positions, unit by unit.

A Turkish artillery battalion passed through our village. I spoke at length with the officers, who said that they're preparing for a large battle. They all seem hopeful. While they're not saying, "We're definitely going to win!" like they did in the past, they're not accepting defeat. A fatherly major said to me, "To be honest, if they'd pursued us after Eskişehir fell, we would've been in bad shape. But they didn't."

A young captain cut in, "They couldn't, because they're more exhausted than us. I think that in a few months they'll stop pushing forward." A younger soldier added, "And that's when we'll launch a counterattack."

In the meantime the villagers had all scampered off and were watching us from a distance.

The major glanced around and asked, "Aren't there any people in this village?"

Without giving me a chance to say anything, the young captain replied, "Sure, but they're all hiding out, just in case. We call 'em village rats."

The major's huge body shook as he laughed. "Soon enough all hell's going to break loose and they'll be scuttling off for sure."

Leaning toward me, the young captain said, "He's right, buddy. You should tell the folks here that it'd be a good idea to round up their animals and head behind the front lines."

I pulled from my pocket one of the leaflets that had been dropped by the Greek airplane and held it out to the captain. "This is what they believe," I said. "They won't listen to me."

As he read the text, his face paled. Thrusting the leaflet to one of his friends, he snarled, "So this is what they believe? In that case, don't tell them anything. These people don't deserve to be saved."

After glancing over the leaflet, the major handed it back to me. Flatly he said, "How could they know better? The enemy hasn't invaded these parts yet. Go tell someone from Thrace that a foreign army or administration could be good. If they don't think you're a traitor, they'll definitely think you're mad. But these people?"

The captain said, "These people? Don't they see what's happening? Haven't they heard? Don't they know what the enemy has done just thirty miles away?"

"How could they?"

"If they don't know, let them stay here and find out."

The major suddenly turned to me. "And you?" he asked. "What are you going to do?"

"Me? I really don't know. I've become like the villagers here. I just leave everything up to fate."

"You can't be serious. While there's still time, make the trip to Ankara . . ."

"Is the danger really that imminent?"

"Of course it is. What do you think is going to happen? If nothing else, this place is going to be caught in the crossfire."

"If nothing else? Is it likely worse will happen? Come on . . ."

I said that without thinking.

The three officers looked at me in astonishment. I don't know if they thought I was mad, but they didn't broach the subject again.

Toward evening they bid me a silent farewell and left.

*

Even though I'd only just met those three officers, I was left with that feeling of melancholy particular to the parting of friends. For hours I sat there feeling dejected.

Such encounters, such coincidences, the coming and going of people from my own class, do nothing but rekindle my feelings of loneliness, and every time I'm left feeling stranger and stranger. That encounter in particular touched me because I knew it was going to be the last time we'd see each other.

Why didn't I talk with them at greater length and in a more sincere, intimate manner? Why didn't I open up and speak to them about my troubles? Why didn't I tell them about the horrific intentions I've been harboring deep down?

Just as someone with cancer is afraid of revealing their tumor, I was afraid of speaking of what's bothering me.

Maybe I did the right thing. If they had found out about my secret, they would've forced me to go with them. They would've hidden me away in some out of the way place behind the front lines like a wounded animal. For nothing I would've been a parasite in the officers' mess halls and tents. Whenever the troops advanced or withdrew, I would've been a burden and a nuisance for the commanders.

Years ago when we were stationed in the desert, there was this tailless dog that became an annoyance for our battalion. No matter where we went, it followed along. It refused to be shooed away and was always trailing behind us. It was constantly trotting around our feet, running around, clambering in and out of the trenches, and sitting in front of various officers' tents at night, keeping guard. We felt sorry for the creature so we couldn't bring ourselves to shoot it. We would even give it our leftovers, which is perhaps why it always stayed with us.

If I'd gone with them, I most certainly would've been like that dog. It's good that I didn't go with them.

It's good that I didn't go with them because every life has its own beginning and end. No one has the power to change that and they shouldn't. Life is indivisible. Can we change its particular and pre-ordained architecture? Do we have that power? And if we were to change it, would the result be something positive, something good?

Starting with my first childhood memories, I envisaged all the aspects of a drama playing out. It was as if I was a silent actor watching myself and acting for myself. I was a tragedian. Now that I'm acting out the last act, am I supposed to suddenly change my role and become a different man?

No. I started like Hamlet, and I'm going to finish like Hamlet.

For me, this is an occupational concern. I can't wipe the dark yellow makeup from my face and repaint it as a lame servant addicted to beatings, a hunchbacked lover, or a frightened old man.

If we can't find a way to live out our lives through our own labor and ideals, we may as well die our own deaths. We don't choose where we're born or who we love, just as we don't have any choice about our faces or our hearts. But we can decide about how we'd like to die.

In the final moment I'm going to use that power, the only power I have. I'm going to die the sweetest and most noble and worthy of deaths.

And I won't be leaving anyone behind, neither friends nor lovers . . . No trace of me will remain, not even a grave, as these villagers won't bury me; they'll leave my body in a stream as fodder for the dogs and crows and burn my bones in their dung fires.

How splendid! In these foreign lands nothing will be left of me, not even my bones.

*

A most extraordinary thing happened in the village today.

I was sitting with a few other people under the vine canopy of the coffeehouse at around noontime. Suddenly a battalion of troops came around the bend in the road in the distance. Nervously, we got up and started walking in their direction. Soon enough we understood that they were our soldiers. That realization, however, did little to soothe the unease of the villagers, or perhaps they were afraid they'd be put to work, but in any case they all scurried off. Bekir Çavuş was also about to leave but I stopped him.

"Wait," I said. "Maybe we can get news from them about what's happening."

Because of the time he served as a soldier, he still bore vestiges of pride in the army.

The battalion made its way along the winding, dusty road. The men weren't marching in formation, however, but rather trudging along in disarray.

Bekir Çavuş watched them for a while and said, "What's this about? There's no front or rear."

Indeed, the group of men resembled neither a troop of soldiers nor a contingent of gendarmes. As they drew nearer, I also noticed that their uniforms and guns were of varying types.

"Hi boys," I said. "Where are you coming from?"

They were so exhausted that, instead of replying, they merely glanced at us with dead eyes framed by eyelashes white with dust.

A few of the men approached us and asked, "Where's the well?"

Gathering his wits, Bekir Çavuş pointed in the direction of the small village square. Some of the soldiers were walking alone, while others scuffled along with two or three others. There was one more trailing along behind the group.

Unable to restrain himself any longer, Bekir Çavuş shouted, "Don't you men have a leader?"

One of the soldiers going to the well turned and pointed to the man walking behind the others.

Stroking his bristly mustache with the back of his hand, Bekir Çavuş tried to compose himself. After peering at the man for a while, he said, "Well just look at that."

As he walked down the road, the sergeant would suddenly stop as if he was lost, look around, and then take a few steps forward.

There really was something strange about him. The way that he was zigzagging across the road gave the impression that he was drunk. He stopped again and looked around, and then he spun around like a

Mevlevi dervish and stopped again, gazing into the distance.

Patience sapped, Bekir Çavuş took a few steps toward him and asked, "Hey buddy, what are you standing there gawking at?"

I saw that he snapped out of his reverie as if startled by the sound of Bekir Çavuş's voice. The sergeant strode up to Bekir Çavuş and the two men stood there, face to face, for a while. Then both of them suddenly cried out and threw their arms around each other.

Curious, I walked up to them. With his hands on the sergeant's shoulders, Bekir Çavuş turned to me and said, "Wonders never cease. You know who this is?"

I scrutinized the man. His skin was tanned as dark as an Indian's and he had a long, graying beard. How old could he be? Maybe thirty, maybe fifty. It's difficult to determine the age of the Anatolian villager—especially if they've spent a long time in the military.

I said, "He must be one of your old friends from the army."

With a smile that was like a cat's yawn, he replied, "This is Şerif. We thought he'd been killed . . . Şerif, Emine's father."

Turning to Şerif, he said, "Your daughter's here in the village, did you know? She got married."

He took a step back in astonishment. "What? Has Emine grown up so much?"

Plunged into thought, he started calculating the years on his fingers . . .

"It's been ten years. That's right, ten years. Back then, she must've been eight."

After a pause, he added, "I wouldn't even recognize her now . . ."

For a minute or so he seemed to be trying to collect his scattered thoughts.

He asked, "Is my mama still alive?"

"Of course, she's in the village."

It was obvious that Emine's father wanted to ask something else. He swallowed and swallowed again. Then he slipped into a strange silence and started looking at us in confusion. The look in his eyes was so bewildered that it seemed the last lights of consciousness had flickered out.

"Sergeant Şerif, let's go to the village."

We started leading him away, but it was like hauling a bashful child off to some strange, new place.

When we reached the coffeehouse, Bekir Çavuş sat him down on a stool and said, "Wait here for a bit."

The soldiers who had gone to the well were lying on the ground nearby, fast asleep.

I said to Emine's father, "Traveler from the afterworld, how do you drink your coffee? Would you like a cigarette?"

When I held out the pack, I noticed that my hand was trembling, as were his.

Sergeant Şerif replied, "Water. Please, some water . . ."

When the keeper of the coffeehouse brought out a large metal cup of water, he picked it up with two hands and started drinking voraciously.

I was becoming increasingly intrigued by this strange "Odysseus," and I watched him closely. Odysseus had also vanished for ten years, though he'd been lost at sea. When he returned to his homeland and encountered his son in a swineherd's hut, neither of them recognized each other at first. In the meantime, his faithful wife Penelope hadn't remarried and was waiting for him at home.

As for the wife of this Anatolian Odysseus, she'd remarried long before. So it was here that Sergeant Şerif's Odysseus was going to be bound in a knot, and a Gordian knot at that.

I couldn't help but wonder: What had he been doing for ten years?

Where had he been? If I were to ask, would he be able to tell his long tale of adventures?

There was always the possibility that he didn't remember anything at all. It seemed that those eventful years had washed over him like water rushing over a rock. But even water leaves traces on the hardest of stones. Is it possible that such a ten-year journey left no mark on the man?

"Sergeant Şerif, where have you been for all these years?"

Staring at a fixed point in front of him, he replied, "In the army . . ."

"Of course, I know you were in the army, but were you taken captive somewhere? No one heard from you for years, what happened?"

"We were captured by the Russians."

"Were you held for a long time? Where were you in Russia?"

"I don't know. They moved us around a lot."

"How did you get back home?"

"I didn't go back home. Ha, today this village just suddenly appeared in front of me. So I knew I was close. I was surprised."

Both of us fell silent for a while.

I asked, "So you're saying you left here ten years ago. Meaning you joined the army before the Balkan War."

"Mm-hmm. When the Balkan War broke out, I was in Rumelia. Then we came to Istanbul. Just as I was being discharged, the army was mobilized again and they sent us to Erzurum."

Again we lapsed into silence. His answers to my consecutive questions were simple, plain, terse. As if he was describing the most unimportant of matters, like "I drank some coffee, I slept, I got up, I washed my face." He described Sarıkamış, Siberian roads and the hunger and misery they suffered, his return on foot and inadvertent crossing of the border, his journey to Kars and how he was then sent east and from there to the south and in the end to Adana. An astounding flow of events that carried him like a piece of driftwood across the face of the world from place to place, bearing him along for thousands of miles. Each wave of this flood lasted months and every sweep in its course took years to traverse.

Sergeant Şerif related the entirety of his saga in just five or ten minutes.

Just then, Bekir Çavuş rounded the corner with Emine in tow, and İsmail was following along behind her.

I said to Sergeant Şerif, "Here comes your daughter."

I'd thought he'd leap up and run towards them. But nothing of the sort happened. He didn't even get to his feet. He merely turned to look in their direction.

Though I was a neutral observer of the events that were transpiring, I was trembling with excitement. The real protagonists, however, contented themselves with a brief hug and Emine leaned down to kiss her father's hand. Afterward, İsmail, who had been standing behind her with his hands tucked into his sash, approached and also kissed his hand.

Bekir Çavuş said, "I couldn't find them at home. I heard they were in the fields so I walked all the way out there. 'Your father's here,' I said. Now you've seen for yourself. Believe me now?"

Emine stood there in silence, timidly scrutinizing her father's features. When her gaze happened to fall on me, she'd cover the side of her face with her headscarf. She was a little plumper than before. But her bare feet, visible beneath her motley-colored skirt, were small, narrow, and delicate, in spite of everything.

What feet for a village woman . . .

I'd never noticed before. As she stood there with one hand on her side, there was such a graceful curve to her waist . . . Where had I seen that pose before? Ah yes, it was an ancient marble relief carving in Pergamon. The woman was wearing a tight, thin dress that buttoned down from the shoulder. As she held that pose, the slight bulge of her thigh was visible, and continuing down, you could see one foot extending out from under her dress. She had small, narrow, delicate feet . . . Just like hers. How strange; just like hers.

Emine was now the sole focus of my attention, and I was blind to all else. Stirred by admiration, I watched this Phrygian sculpture that seemed to have been freshly pried from the earth. My eyes were devouring her from head to foot. With a single glance I took in her round shoulders, the sweet curves of her hands, and all that was below her waist as well.

She probably sensed that I was gazing at her. She was constantly shifting position; first standing in such a way that I could only see her profile, then turning her back completely, and then taking cover behind Bekir Çavuş. Poor girl, if only she knew how heartfelt my glances were . . . Yet there was something in her movements, in her expressions and body language, that consoled me. She didn't appear to love İsmail in the least.

When a woman is bound to her man, it's obvious from a single look. How, you ask? It's quite easy to sense but difficult to explain. But I could feel it. Even if I were to ask Emine why she was so disinterested in İsmail, why she was so repulsed by him, she wouldn't be able to account for it. This is not a matter of the intellect. In the depths of the spirit it's something more internal: A blind, deaf, mute, and dark thing. She wants you, she doesn't. She loves you, she doesn't. And yet we become her obedient pawn.

If I were to ask Emine . . . She knelt down beside her father. A kitten couldn't be tamer. So why does she become so wild and skittish, like a frightened game animal, when it comes to me? Because I am a stranger. I can't help but wonder if this social isolation, which, for the Anatolian villager, holds sway over both sexuality and the instincts, is an effect of these desolate plains, which themselves summon souls to loneliness and seclusion?

Or does it arise from some flaw in the social order?

As these thoughts flitted through my mind, I went on exploring Emine with my eyes. At one point our gazes seemed to collide. Her expression was akin to that of a child caught in the grip of mischievous arms and longing to slip free . . . But I didn't let go for a second. I squeezed her tighter and tighter in the confines of my imprisoning gaze. In the end, however, my obstinacy started to make her laugh. In a sense, she was preoccupied with me. I was pleading and she was fleeing. As I threatened her, she toyed with me.

I don't know how long that went on. Sergeant Şerif suddenly leapt to his feet.

"I'm going," he said, "to see my mother."

For someone like Sergeant Şerif who has travelled the globe, of what significance is the distance between two villages? Immediately he set off and Emine went with him, so İsmail had no choice but to trail along behind them. Bekir Çavuş stayed with me.

Before they got very far, the three-person caravan stopped. Emine's father turned to us and shouted, "Tell the troops I'll be back before the hour's up."

Bekir Çavuş replied, "You can't make it back that soon!"

When the sergeant set off down the road again, Bekir Çavuş called out, "If you're late, should I send the troops on their way?"

Sergeant Şerif turned and gestured as if to say, "It's up to you."

Bekir Çavuş shouted, "Wait! Where are they going?"

We could barely hear the sergeant's reply: "Polatlı! Polatlı!"

Sergeant Şerif never returned to our village. The next morning Emine and İsmail found out that the soldiers had already left. Neither of them said a word about the sergeant.

Grinning slyly, Bekir Çavuş said, "I knew it. He never planned on coming back." Emine and İsmail merely hung their heads in silence.

It pained me to see a ten-year adventure undertaken—even if unintentionally—for the sake of the homeland come to such an abrupt end. Unable to restrain myself, I said, "Tell him that he needs to rejoin his troops. Otherwise it won't bode well for him."

After Emine and İsmail left, Bekir Çavuş said to me, "What's it to you! Everything's a mess, so who cares?"

Have we really reached that point? If so, why is the Anatolian army preparing for another battle on the other side of those mountains? Why are those great Turkish commanders who've never suffered a defeat bolstering the front lines?

I'm burning with a desire to go see for myself. I want to travel to the battlefront as if it were the Kaaba and circumambulate its tents.

Is there any other place to which all Turks could go?

All Turks? No, I meant to say all oppressed people. The impoverished have been left foodless so that the wealthy statesmen of a few greedy Western countries can eat four meals a day. Countless homes have been set ablaze and countless households have been brought to ruin. Now the Anatolian villager with his cracked heels is being flushed out and hunted down under the orders of the pink-skinned lord of Westminster. But can a filet of steak be carved from a villager's breast? They're all just skin and bone.

As I was thinking about such matters, Süleyman, whom I hadn't seen in a long time, suddenly showed up at my door. He stood before me, typifying the destitute Anatolian peasant I'd been envisaging just moments before, clad in rags that barely covered his body. His arms were mere sticks and his head a skull with embers for eyes.

"Ah, Süleyman, where have you been?"

Out of fear I couldn't bring myself to look him in the face as I spoke. When he replied, it was an incomprehensible groan. What's that? Where? At home, ill? What's wrong? Malaria? Nonstop coughing? Hacking all night long. A fever, a fever . . .

"Can't swallow anything but water."

After a fit of coughing, he added, "I'm a bit better now. But if I could have some hot soup, I'd get my strength back."

"Let me boil up a nice chicken for you."

He grinned strangely, his thirty-two teeth seeming to suddenly jut from his skull. Pained by the state he was in, I bowed my head.

"Süleyman, have a seat. Let me check your pulse."

Looking at my watch, I held his outstretched wrist. 110 beats per minute.

"And let me check your temperature."

103 degrees.

"Süleyman, you need to get some rest now. Here. You'll stay in Emeti Kadın's room. Lie down and rest."

"I don't want to. I'm fine."

When I insisted, he said he was going to go back home.

"Fine, go home. I'll send you some soup. But don't go out and walk around. You'll get worse."

He didn't believe me.

"But I don't have any aches."

While we were talking, Salih Ağa's hunchbacked son came limping up and sat down with us. His face was also as yellow as saffron. He had dark circles around his eyes and his nose drooped towards his mouth like a thick beak.

"I ache all over," he said, and, pointing to his left thigh, he added, "There's something wrong here too."

"What seems to be wrong?"

Balling his hand into a fist, he said, "A tumor about this big."

"Hasn't your father done anything?"

"I've told him again and again. But he doesn't care. My mama she put some hot things on it but it just got worse. If I had a donkey, I'd go to town and see a doctor."

It was obvious he was trying to get my donkey. I pretended not to understand.

Wait, what was that? Thunder? No, it couldn't be. Not in this weather. I looked around. There wasn't a cloud in the sky. All the same, I knew that thunder and lightning can happen even when the sky is seemingly clear. I sat and listened. No, it didn't sound like thunder.

Far in the distance there were occasional, irregular booms.

A cool morning breeze was blowing and the plains were calm. Out in the fields everyone was going about their work. I went out for a stroll by myself.

As I walked to the south of the village, it seemed like the faint booms were slightly louder. Climbing to the top of a small rise, I listened as intently as I could.

It was none other than the sound of cannons. But how distant were they? I made calculations, using a formula I'd learned during the war. The distance the sound travelled depended on the size of the cannon. But at the same time, the weather conditions have to be taken into account, and the direction of the wind can throw the calculations completely off. In any case, the sound I was hearing was indisputably cannons.

"Doom . . ."

That word fell from my lips. I don't know what I meant by it. A heaviness settled over my thoughts. I was saying "Doom" and finding myself caught between a bizarre feeling of joy and deep melancholy.

I've heard cannons up close and seen them as well. I saw how, on the other side of the trenches, their long, dark barrels rise and fall with every shot fired and I heard the sound of shells, like a violent tearing of cloth that is thunderously loud. While I lost my right arm as the result of a bullet wound, countless times shells soared over my head and flew past to my right and left, and countless times I was caught in hails of shrapnel. But none of that filled me with as much dread as the distant roar of those cannons.

I slumped down on a rock. The desolate plain spread out before me in countless, motionless waves of earth, looking like a frozen, barren sea. On that sweep of land which stretched to the horizon there were no trees, clumps of bushes, glimmering ponds, animals, or buildings.

It was as though life had abandoned this place for all eternity and I was alone in a dead world. I once peered at the moon through a telescope at an observatory; as I looked out from that rocky rise in Central Anatolia, the view was one and the same.

And the sound of those distant guns lent a horrific grandeur to the scene, leaving me with the sinking feeling that I was bearing witness to the approach of an apocalypse. One of the many tales of divine wrath and punishment depicted in Torahic legend now seemed to be unfolding apace.

I wondered: What am I doing here? Am I the last inhabitant, the last living creature, of this dead world? No . . . I suppose not.

A herd of sheep came over the top of the hill opposite me and started descending its slope. Soon after Hasan's spindly silhouette appeared at the top of the hill, twig-like against the backdrop of the sky. It was odd. My heart was cheered, as if that herd and shepherd were bringing me glad tidings. Getting to my feet, I signaled to him and shouted as loudly as I could, "Hasan, come over here. Hasan . . ."

But he was too far away to hear me. I decided to sit and wait. The herd continued to slowly make its way down the hill, leaving a white trail in the parched earth as it zigzagged right and left, forward and back, like a huge string of prayer beads in nervous hands. I don't know what those poor animals find to eat in these barren lands. Can those thistles growing among the stones be considered forage?

Most likely Hasan heard me eventually, because he stopped and seemed to prick up his ears. When I got up and signaled to him again, he started heading in my direction.

The booming of the cannons continued at irregular intervals, but I couldn't tell if it was closer or farther away than a little while ago. Probably farther, based on my estimations. As if the enemy had moved to a new position in the last hour. But if that were the case, the sound of the cannons would've stopped until the enemy established its new position. Who's to say, however, that those were enemy cannons? Perhaps it was our troops who had been firing shells since morning.

Lost in thought, I didn't even notice Hasan approaching until he was standing right in front of me.

"Hasan, do you hear the sound of those cannons?"

"Since morning I been hearing something. But cannons? I don't know. I thought there was a storm somewhere far off."

"No, Hasan. Those are cannons."

The little shepherd didn't seem to grasp the meaning of the word. Cannons or thunder . . . For him, there mustn't have been much difference between the two.

"Hasan, there's a war going on behind those hills."

"What does war mean?"

"A fight between armies . . ."

At that moment we heard the distant sound of the propellers of four or five airplanes. We peered up into the sky. As if frightened of the sound of the cannons, those huge bird-machines seemed to be fleeing in our direction.

Still looking up with his mouth agape, Hasan said, "Wow, it's just like the buzzing of bees . . ."

The airplanes were flying on a fixed course and since they were getting smaller and smaller, it was apparent that their destination was somewhere to the northeast of us. As they flew off, they increased in altitude to the point that we could no longer hear them, and they were now mere black dots in the sky.

The little shepherd said, "They didn't throw down any papers this time."

At that moment, there was a burst of sparks followed by a strange crackling. A few minutes later there was another rain of sparks and more crackling.

Hands on his hips as he gazed up, Hasan exclaimed, "They threw down some fire!"

He seemed greatly entertained, and there wasn't a trace of fear or concern in his expression. On the contrary, his eyes were ablaze with curiosity, as if he was seeing a new children's game for the first time.

I surmised that the airplanes were targeting our headquarters and I was waiting for our troops to return fire. But when their bombs were spent, the airplanes merely flew a half-circle and headed back in the direction from which they'd come, though I got the impression a few shots were fired at them as they flew off.

Hasan was getting more excited by the minute, exclaiming "Wow, wow!" and his mouth still hanging open. I was trying to explain the situation to him but in vain, as he didn't hear a word I said. Who knows what tales he was spinning in his mind in an attempt to grasp this extraordinary situation . . .

*

In the days that followed, the cannon fire and flyovers of airplanes became increasingly frequent, to the point that the villagers have started to feel a modicum of fear. But when I say to them, "Let's leave," they ignore me. One of them asked, "So what are *you* waiting for?"

Indeed, what am I waiting for? I am incapable of explaining that to myself. My hands and feet move just fine. But my will which commands them to move seems to have been paralyzed. I'm unable to make decisions, and my sense of prudence is shackled.

That happens sometimes during dreams. You want to shout, but your voice sticks in your throat; you want to run, but your legs won't budge.

One day Bekir Çavuş said to me, "Look, it won't do any good to scare these people. They've already lost heart. If they get panicked, they'll all run off. But this is the harvest time. They'd regret it."

True, the entire year's harvest is lying in small heaps in the fields. How could they leave it behind? The entire year's harvest . . . That, for the villager, is the one and only concern in life. Nothing else in the world could be of greater importance.

I said to Bekir Çavuş, "You're right, I won't say a word more."

As I spoke those words, I felt like my heart was transformed into the obedient heart of a child. I'd lost all authority over both myself and others. A villager could object to my assertions. He could give me advice and I'd comply. "You're right," I'd say, because my knowledge was no longer of use. My hopes had been for naught. My predictions had been wrong. My logic had foundered in the face of their instincts and common sense.

I now see them with a newfound respect and sense of obeisance. With his notorious grin, Salih Ağa strikes me as being the embodiment of wit and acumen, and when I look at his bare feet, I see a reflection of a truth so lofty that it's far beyond my reach. And Zeynep Kadın, who holds nothing in high regard and speaks to no one as she busies herself piling hay on the flat roof of her house, appears to me as a symbol of vitality worthy of the deepest admiration. I can't even bring myself to look at her stern, dour face.

In her presence, I feel that I'm overly anxious and frantic, as if at any moment she'll slap me and say, "Now you just sit in a corner somewhere and shut up!"

As for Süleyman, he bears the nobleness of the otherworldly and matters of this realm no longer concern him. On occasion when I probe him about the issue of heaven, I sense that he is perplexed. He doesn't grin when I say the word "heaven" as he did in the past, nor do his eyes glimmer; he merely looks at me with uncomprehending disinterest.

If Memiş were here, perhaps it would be possible to find a companion in him. But he disappeared two months ago, and no one knows where he went. The recent inauspicious occurrences have been attributed to his disappearance. When I first showed up at the village all the blame was pinned on me, but now his departure has made everyone forget my arrival.

Although I said to Bekir Çavuş, "You're right, I won't say a word more," I feel a desperate need to talk. It's tearing at my heart. I want to talk to the stones, to the earth. What's the difference between them and Zeynep Kadın's severe face? Do they even want me here?

Nature, you are harsh and rugged. As I said, you are like the bosom of a stepmother. I feel that truth now more than ever before. You offer neither shade where I can find a fleeting sense of peace, nor waters along the banks of which I can cool off! Hard-hearted earth! When my body falls upon you, never to rise again, with what wild brutality will you press me to your breast?

*

Yesterday we could hear the faraway sound of the cannons and a few airplanes passed by in the distance. The smell of gunpowder now fills the air. We hear the sound of plane engines more than the braying of donkeys or barking of dogs.

The villagers enjoy watching the airplanes fly overhead. Leaning against the wall, they gaze upward open-mouthed and exclaim, "Wow, wow, wow!" "Did you see that one? It's even bigger." "No, that one's bigger." "The one in front's flying faster." "That one's going slow." And when one of the planes looks like it's going to nosedive, they cry out, "My God, it's going to crash!"

As if the plane on the verge of crashing was a mere plaything . . . I become so enraged that I can't sit still. If I had a proper rifle, I'd stand in the middle of the village and take shots at those smug airplanes. But all I have is a double-barreled shotgun and a Browning pistol.

One day, even though I'd given Bekir Çavuş my word, I snapped, "You shouldn't be standing around gawking at the enemy planes. It's a disgrace."

Someone in the crowd piped up, "Why not? They're not doing anything to us."

Grumbling, they started to disperse. But Salih Ağa remained behind. He shuffled up to me and, though he was grinning, I could tell he was somewhat intimidated. He said, "You say that but them planes been helpful. Didn't you notice that the crows don't come around? Used to be they'd come eat our grain during the harvest."

I turned and glared at him, freezing him in his tracks. Like the day when I beat him, he started wheezing. I walked off, leaving him standing there.

One day the pilots of the planes tossed down some more leaflets.

The villagers were running around picking them up as if they were manna falling from the sky. At first they tried to read them, but when that failed they folded the leaflets up and tucked them into their sashes like good luck charms.

Some of them went to the imam and asked, "Read this, what's it say?"

The imam started reading, syllable by syllable: "Esteemed village residents, the Kemalist bandits have been crushed. One by one we are taking over all the cities and towns. Now we are marching on Ankara. Do not engage in hostile acts. We were sent by the Caliphate to save you."

"What does it mean?"

" . . .We were sent by the Caliphate to save you."

They knew nothing about the Caliphate or the Prophet, for that matter. But they liked the part about being saved, though they didn't really understand it. Saved! Who could possibly save you people? Not even angels from the heavens could save you, because first you need to be saved from yourselves. That's what I was muttering to myself before I snatched the leaflet out of the imam's hand and ground it on the floor with the heel of my boot.

Everyone looked at me in astonishment.

Was I going crazy? Or was it some kind of fit? Most likely I was afflicted by a mental imbalance. The fact that I'd become so desperate that I meekly complied with Bekir Çavuş's admonitions and then put on a show of bravery by grabbing the leaflet from the imam probably meant that my state of mind was anything but normal.

Given the circumstances, however, wouldn't it be abnormal to be normal? Every era has its own particular standards. If living like the world is at peace during times of war and boxing oneself into static paradigms when a revolution is underway isn't indicative of negligence, indolence, or perversion, what is it?

My mind is swarming with contradictory thoughts and conflicting notions. These days, as I sense that the final moments of my life are drawing near, I've been trying to better comprehend myself but my efforts have been in vain. Whenever I attempt to pin it down, my own sense of self vanishes under my hands in a puff of smoke. I've also been trying to make sense of the world around me. But again, it's a pointless endeavor . . . The world is as dumb as it is deaf. In recent times, my environs have become so closed off, so obscured, I don't know what I should be looking or listening for. It's as though I myself have become the enemy and this place is a castle that refuses to surrender.

If this little community could speak as one, it would say, "Yes, *you* are the enemy!" Isn't that what the eyes of the people are saying? Isn't that what they're expressing through their actions and behavior? For them, I'm not just an objectionable guest and a brazen parasite, I'm a malignancy that brings bad luck. They'll hold me personally responsible for just about everything that goes wrong. That's how angry and hostile they've become.

One day Bekir Çavuş said to me with a glare in his eye, "The enemy was way over in Izmir. But those bandits attacked them left and right, never letting up. They're the reason why the enemy has moved in this far. I don't know what to say. Damn them all . . ."

I wanted nothing more than to slap him across the face, but I held myself back. For the last time I tried to enlighten him about the unity of the homeland: "For a Turk, Izmir and Sivas are one and the same, just as Diyarbakır and Samsun are one and the same. If Izmir falls, all of Anatolia falls too. So long as that city remains in the hands of the enemy, you can't liberate these lands either."

Bekir Çavuş cut me off, saying, "Oh come on . . . Save it for someone else."

I snapped, "Bekir Çavuş, if you don't come to your senses, I'll knock some sense into you."

Quickly he composed himself, most likely recalling our difference in rank.

"My apologies. We're just villagers and we don't understand things like this." He got up to leave but I grabbed him by the arm, pulling him back down.

"You're not just a villager. You were once a soldier, and saying such things doesn't befit a soldier. It's a disgrace, I say, a disgrace!"

A soldier! Yes, but a soldier in an army that had been routed. If a man's spirits have been crippled by the blunt force of countless blows, it's impossible to rouse them again. Trying to instill in Bekir Çavuş a feeling of epic enthusiasm was particularly futile and untimely given the fact that the enemy was already in control of the nearby hills.

He said, "But I know, sir, that you are one of them."

"One of who?"

"Kemal Pasha's supporters."

"How could one be a Turk and not be one of his supporters?"

"Sir, we're not Turks."

"What are you then?"

"We're Muslims, praise be to God . . . *Those* people live in Haymana."

I lacked the strength to go on discussing the matter with him. As I slipped into despair, my head fell to my chest like a man who's been hung.

Even if we are destined for victory, all we're going to save are these arid plains and hills. Where are the people? They don't yet exist. We'll have to create them anew with these Bekir Çavuşes, Salih Ağas, Zeynep Kadıns, İsmails, and Süleymans.

If I didn't back Kemal Pasha, who else could I support? He's the leader of those self-sacrificing heroes who will succeed in completing the grand task that lies ahead of us. Even though the booming cannons are just fifteen miles away, I still believe we'll prevail. All the same, however, there will be a second round of battles and their conclusion seems as distant and nebulous as fanciful tales of legend.

Bekir Çavuş apologized again. "I'm sorry, sir," he said, "but I can't stop thinking about the rumor that's going around."

I knew he wanted me to ask about the rumor. When I didn't respond, he went on: "You know Salih Ağa's son? Well, he's brought our daughter to ruin. I said to him, 'Marry her!' but he refuses, saying that he's got a tumor in his right leg, that his whole body aches. It's all lies. If he's so sick, how could he do what he did?"

I'd been the first witness to the tragedy. I couldn't help but ask, "What does your daughter say about all this?"

"What can she say? He tricked her, saying they'd get married. For a long time now he's been using her as if they were engaged. We only found out about it later."

"She's not pregnant, is she?"

"No, she can't be. She's only twelve."

*

One morning—I'll never forget that morning!—I heard a voice outside, just below my window. A high-pitched, piercing child's voice.

"They're coming! They're coming!"

Leaping out of bed, I ran in the direction of the voice.

"Hasan, who's coming?"

The little shepherd was panting for breath and his face was pale, either out of fright or because he'd run all the way to the village.

"Them . . . The ones you talked about . . . They're coming over the pass."

At first I couldn't pull my thoughts together, and I stood there staring blankly at Hasan.

"I left the herd over on the hill," he said. "I have to go back." With that, he ran off.

I paced around my room in confusion like a man who suddenly finds that his house is burning down around him. As I searched for my boots and my vest, I kept unbuttoning and then re-buttoning my pajamas, but in the end I had to call out for help.

"Emeti Kadın! Emeti Kadın!"

There was no reply. I dashed out and checked the hallway, kitchen, rooftop, stable. She was nowhere to be found. I ran over to the chicken coop. She wasn't there either. It was unthinkable that she hadn't shown up by that time.

Still wearing my pajamas and slippers, I ran all the way to her house and knocked on her door. No one answered. It was as if everyone in the village was still asleep, even the children and animals.

Only a few dogs that saw me running around in that bizarre outfit started barking.

By that point I couldn't bring myself to go back home. Bewildered, I began knocking on the doors of all the houses but they were as silent as tombs. In the hope of finding someone, I went as far as the square but the entire village was eerily desolate.

From the square I could see the road that Hasan had mentioned. And what did I see? A cloud of dust rising into the air as the enemy troops marched toward the village. I ran home, glancing back over my shoulder.

As I struggled to get dressed, I was thinking about the villagers. Were they all hiding out in their homes? Or had they fled? The fact that the enemy was approaching troubled me little, as I was more concerned about answering those two questions. I wondered if they'd made a secret agreement and run off together, leaving me to face the enemy alone . . . Ultimately, however, I deemed it unlikely that they would stoop to such treachery and cowardice.

And in any case, where would they go? Everyone had been around the night before, and I doubted they could've heard that the enemy was approaching before little Hasan spotted the troops. No, they couldn't have fled. They must've been hunkered down in their houses.

I sensed that the soldiers were about to enter the village. The clattering of a heavy gun carriage filled the air as an artillery battery moved down the road. Instinctively I locked my door and closed the shutters on my windows. Why? Even now I'm incapable of explaining that to myself.

But I was going to put on my military uniform and face down the enemy with my sword, wasn't I? Come now, I was all alone. Would I be the only one who was spared all those approaching perils? What need was there to force cruelty and oppression upon myself?

But those precautions I'd taken! They suddenly made no sense. I unlocked the door and opened the windows. The sound of horse hooves, carriages, and clanking metal was getting louder by the second, and I caught the pungent smell of rust and leather mixed with dust.

A strange clamor was rising up from the village as people's voices joined the tumult, just like in my nightmares. I could hear words like, "Vire, İstaso, Vire, Palikari . . ."

This peculiar Turkish village huddled in a distant corner of Anatolia, heretofore cut off from the rest of the world, was now stirring with the commotion of a Port of Piraeus . . .

And not a word of Turkish was heard.

I broke out in a cold sweat. My ears were ringing. I didn't have the strength in my legs to stand. It felt as though I'd been sliced in half at the waist with a razor-sharp sword.

For a moment I wondered if they'd come to set me ablaze like a dried out log . . .

Then I heard a voice call out in Turkish, "Hey, isn't there anyone in this village?"

The accent made me think of Istanbul's Galata district. The inflection, however, wasn't quite like how the Greeks of Istanbul speak Turkish. It could've been an Armenian, or perhaps a Jewish person. There's something disheartening about hearing Turkish spoken in such a manner, as if the language is being dismembered. It feels like your body is being mauled by cruel, insolent hands that reach deep down inside you and tear at your most tender parts with jagged fingernails.

"Isn't there anyone here?"

They started banging on the doors of the houses but there still wasn't a peep from the villagers. If only those soldiers knew that I was just as curious as them . . . I could hear footsteps approaching my house and then people talking below my window. When I peered outside, I saw that someone was looking in at me. A dark-skinned young man with a long, curling mustache and beard stubble. We stared at each other for a few moments. After looking around my room in surprise, he withdrew. I'm not sure how much time passed, but next I heard the sound of boots clomping around in my house.

The door of my room swung open and the young man I'd seen a few minutes earlier strode inside. In the same Turkish I'd heard before, he asked, "What's going on in this village? There's no one around. Aren't you from here?"

I shook my head in the negative.

"Very well, but don't you know where everyone is?"

Again I shook my head no.

A few more soldiers entered my room, rifles at the ready. The man with the mustache turned and spoke to them in Greek, and then they all looked at me, suddenly curious. Mechanically they gazed at my empty sleeve and then at my face.

"You mute or what? Why don't you tell me where the others are?"

"I'll tell you when I feel like it."

Irritably he turned back to the others and said something I surmised was derogatory. Furious, I leapt to my feet and snarled, "What right do you have to come into my bedroom? And what gives you the authority to interrogate me like this?"

The young man glanced at his friends as if to say, "Didn't I tell you so? This guy's a lunatic."

I shouted, "Whether I'm mad or not, you're going to leave. Immediately!"

As though he was talking to a simpleton, he replied, "Okay, fine, we'll leave, we'll go. But first tell me. Where are the villagers?"

I stood there, defiantly silent. Running out of patience, he started to leave with the others, but not before ordering one of the soldiers to fix his bayonet and stand guard.

Now that they were gone, I wanted to close my bedroom door but the soldier wouldn't allow it. So in order to put on certain airs, I sat down in my armchair and started to read.

Outside there were more people coming and going, more shouts, more clamoring. A few times I heard doors being smashed open.

Then I started to hear the sound of the villagers' voices amidst the commotion, which meant they'd made do with locking themselves inside their homes. Such pitiful, naive people. Did you really think the enemy could be fooled so easily?

*

For the last few days the village has been occupied by enemy troops. While not all of them are staying in the village proper, all of the higher-ranking officers and commanders have seized houses for themselves. I say officers and commanders, but I've never seen their faces nor do I know precisely what rank they hold, with one exception. Emeti Kadın is my only source of news, as I hardly ever leave my room.

I asked her, "Where were you on the first day?"

"When my son came running and told us what was happening, everyone met up in front of the mosque. Salih Ağa and Bekir Çavuş said, 'All the girls, women, and children should take whatever they can and hide out by the creek. The rest of us will lock ourselves inside and stay quiet. Maybe the soldiers will leave if they don't see anyone.' So that's what we did. But soon we heard that the enemy wasn't hurting people. They don't do anything because they want everyone to come back. All they want is meat, bread, barley, and sugar. They say they'll pay for it. Look at this. They took some milk and eggs from me but they gave me these."

She pulled out a few pieces of paper that had been tightly folded up like good luck charms. Holding them out to me, she asked, "What do they say?"

There were a few lines written in pencil.

"I don't know. It's Greek. But I can tell you that it's not worth anything."

Emeti Kadın gulped.

"What? Well, what should I do now?"

"Emeti Kadın, you shouldn't have given them anything in the first place."

"How can I say no? They come right into my house and wait by the coop. When a chicken gets up, they grab any eggs that're there and leave. I can't chase after them."

On the first day, they ransacked my house on the pretext they were looking for weapons. When they found my guns, they went on searching, even rifling a few times through the drawer where I keep my money. Using their bayonets, they tore up my mattress, pillows, and everything else with stuffing, and they threw all my books and papers into a pile in the middle of the room.

I stood leaning against the wall, nonchalantly watching the soldiers. One of them picked up this notebook and flipped through it, trying to read what I'd written, but in the end he tossed it back on my desk. Another one was jotting down the names of my French books in a pocket notepad. When they were finished, they said they were going to take me to see their commander.

"Why?" I asked. "I refuse to go."

"If you don't go with us willingly, we'll take you by force."

I thought about it. Resistance seemed futile, so I fell into step in front of the soldiers. The sergeant who spoke Turkish was walking beside me.

"You're an officer," he said. "You're not even from this village. What are you doing here? Why did you come to this place?" He said I'd have to explain myself to the commander.

I had neither hat nor jacket as I walked down the road, the right sleeve of my shirt tied into a large knot that swung with each step I took.

I walked on. The few villagers I saw on the streets turned away as soon as they caught sight of me. There were so many horses, draft mules, and water buffalo that I had to push my way past them. One of the commander's first orders of business had been to turn the coffeehouse into his headquarters, and he was now sitting there behind a large table under the vine canopy. He was a dour-faced captain doing his utmost to cut an imposing figure.

When the sergeant said something and pointed me out, the captain looked up and scrutinized my face. In French he asked, "You're an officer, correct?"

"Yes."

"Please sit down and answer each of the questions I put to you."

When the interrogation was complete, the enemy commander still could not comprehend why I would leave Istanbul of my own free will and settle in this village. My psychological explanations failed to persuade him of my motivations, as did my most candid admissions, and he went on eyeing me with suspicion. I proved to be a rather prickly, insoluble issue for him. Ultimately he decided to shuffle off the problem by saying, "Go back home. But from now on, you are not to go out or speak to anyone. That's all for now."

When I got back to my room, I saw no point in tidying up. I started living like a drenched rat in all that disorder and tumult.

There's a soldier standing at the front door of my house, a bayonet affixed to his rifle.

Who knows how many more days I will be able to write in this notebook.

*

The enemy doesn't give me a moment of peace, not even when I'm sleeping. They keep me under constant surveillance, watching me through my windows and from the doorway. Given this state of affairs, the only time I can write in my notebook is after midnight when everyone has retired for the evening and the soldier on watch dozes off. Then I slip into bed and, as a precaution, put out the lamp, meaning that these lines have been scrawled in the dark, much like how the Italian poet d'Annunzio wrote *Nocturne* bereft of sight. Lucky is he who can read what I've written here.

In fact, I do want people to read my observations because certain aspects of the war of Anatolia, this great calamity and saga known as the struggle for independence, will not go down in history. Indeed, they have only been recorded here, so if some perfidious hand takes an eraser to these sinuous lines written in pencil, future generations will be deprived of knowledge about some of the painful realities that afflicted this country.

This is no longer my story. Even those sections about my experiences are depicted as though they'd been lived out by someone else. Imagine that I, an officer named Ahmet Celâl, am merely the specter of a crippled war veteran, and in the dead of night I crawl into his empty bed to narrate what has transpired.

Poor Ahmet Celâl has died and demons of hell await him at his grave. But to tell the truth, I don't know if the torment of the afterlife has started for him yet. If you'd like, take that remark about the demons of hell to mean the initiation of his suffering, as he lived his life in this world as if it were purgatory. He never knew what kind of god he worshipped. For years he fought and spilled his blood for a foreign empire. For years he burned with longing for an unknown country, for an ideal homeland. For years he sought out an intangible, invisible love, for the sake of which he wept, laughed, and made grand pronouncements, but when it was time for him to move on to the next world, he came to see it was all lies.

That was more painful than everything else. Discovering that his entire life had signified nothing, realizing that he had squandered his youth pursuing empty dreams, hollow aspirations, and misguided endeavors, and at the last moment coming face to face with the vilest and most horrific realities . . . Before suffering the anguish of the otherworld, Ahmet Celâl was surely seared by the flames of truth. He consorted with those demons. If anything, that's why you should take pity on him.

*

The enemy troops are still exploiting the people. But this decrepit village is possessed of such an essence that it has been able to feed all those men since their arrival. Emeti Kadın never seems to run out of eggs. And based on what I've heard, the enemy's draft animals have yet to finish off Salih Ağa's stores of hay and barley. Along with their families, Bekir Çavuş and Zeynep Kadın are constantly carrying sacks of cracked wheat, beans, and chickpeas to the kitchens of the various command posts around the village, and every day one or two sheep disappear from Hasan's herd.

Regardless of what they take, the officers and soldiers always say, "We're going to pay for it." As Emeti Kadın gets more and more slips of paper covered in Greek writing, the less she believes she'll actually get paid. A few days ago I asked quietly, "If that's the case, why do you keep them?"

"Everyone does, so I do too. Maybe they'll pay us in the end."

"It's pointless," I said. "Just tear them up and throw them away."

She frowned, seemingly on the brink of tears.

"Oh I couldn't do that. It would be wrong. They'd beat me."

Lowering my voice even more, I asked, "Beat you? Have they been beating others?"

"A lot. Really a lot. If you don't give them what they want, they make like they're going to hit you."

Speaking in little more than a whisper, I pressed her further: "Have they been violating the honor of the women here, Emeti Kadın?"

"So far not much. They bother some of the girls sometimes, but I never seen it myself. Zeynep Kadın told me."

My voice now a mere breath of air, I asked, "How does she know?"

"They harass the girls a lot. They can't even go to the well or go out to wash laundry anymore."

No longer could I bring myself to ask specifically about Emine. In any case, the guard watching us through the window of my room was starting to get suspicious because we were whispering to each other. He was staring at me as if he was trying to read my lips.

But this morning . . . I can't believe it. Even now I still can't believe my eyes. I went outside and there wasn't a single enemy soldier in sight. They'd left. But where did they go? Salih Ağa and the imam were nowhere to be found. I was told that the commander had met with the villagers early in the morning and said, "I need two men to serve as guides. We're going to press onward, but we'll come back. So keep the tallies we gave you. When we return, we'll pay what we owe."

Salih Ağa and the imam immediately stepped forward, saying, "We'll show you the way."

As she was telling me about it, Emeti Kadın was shaking her head. "He's a sly one, that Salih Ağa," she said. "He did that 'cause he hopes to get paid for his hay and barley."

"How could he? They said they'd pay when they get back."

"Oh he'll get it. He'll trick them somehow. If we're going to get our money, that's the only way. As if we believe they'll come back . . . Who's going to come back, who's going to pay up? It's not going to happen."

"I tried to warn you. Only now you're coming to your senses."

Emeti Kadın thought for a moment and said, "From now on, if anyone asks I'm going to tell them to pay up front. If they don't, not a single egg or a drop of milk for them."

"Hopefully," I said, "no one will come asking for anything."

I didn't really believe what I was saying, however, because the enemy troops are advancing, not retreating. This is the tenth day of the recent offensive. After all this time, whatever happens is inevitable.

The fact that the enemy is driving forward can only mean that the war is tipping in their favor. If that's true, they're marching on Ankara. But will they occupy our new capital city? It's inconceivable. Such a turn of events would run contrary to the logic of historical developments because Ankara represents a fresh start, not the end of an era.

This city, which is now mentioned alongside Moscow and London in telegrams being sent around the world, stands in a class of its own. It has become a symbol of a new spirit, a new vitality.

The enemy could invade the mud-brick city of Ankara that can be found on old maps. A few cannonballs would be enough to destroy it. But how could they encroach upon the spirit that bears the same name? How could they seize it? If that spirit thrives here today, it will blow like the wind there tomorrow, and the next day it will be whipped into a storm and find an even higher, craggier peak where it will thunder and roar. Woe to he who doesn't grasp that truth now, for soon enough he will lament his folly and lose his way on precipitous slopes.

I write these lines even though Emeti Kadın is once again awaiting the return of the enemy. I write these lines as the enemy troops are launching an attack on the far side of Sakarya, a mere forty miles from Ankara.

Salih Ağa and the imam returned ten days later. In spite of my feelings of animosity, I couldn't resist the urge to speak with them, and my sense of curiosity drove me into the presence of those two wretches. Neither of them, however, would say a word at first. Salih Ağa was aggrieved because he didn't get paid for his hay and barley, and the other—perhaps—was vexed because he didn't get tipped for his services. I say that because they mentioned their own interests during the course of our tense conversation.

"How far did you go?"

They said the name of a place I've never heard of and fell silent for a while.

"Chaos, pure chaos. The cannons are so loud it's unbearable."

"They've been fighting for three days and three nights."

"What about the enemy? Is their morale up?"

"They seem pessimistic . . ."

Salih Ağa cut off the imam by saying, "Not true. That soldier who can speak Turkish said, 'We'll be in Ankara in a few days!'"

"A few days?" I asked. "Even if they marched nonstop it would take longer than that."

Shooting me a dark look, Salih Ağa sneered, "You'll see."

"Tell me, what am I going to see? You saw for yourself. They went through all your hay and barley and then didn't pay you anything after making you walk for days as their guide."

He started shaking his bare foot more violently than I'd ever seen before.

Reproachfully he snapped, "Yeah, yeah. Got anything else to say?"

Never before had he spoken to me so brusquely, and he only dared do so because he sensed that the clout I represented was retreating from these lands.

"You scoundrel," I snarled, "even if those backstabbers you trust so much were here, I'd still grind you under my boot like the dirty snake you are."

When I stormed up to him, he faced me down and said, "No, those days are over. Sit back down."

Rearing back, I slapped him across his grizzled face as hard as I could, sending him sprawling to the ground, but he was back on his feet in an instant. He picked up a large stone which he proceeded to hurl at me, but it only grazed my shoulder.

Now standing in a circle around us, the villagers looked on. Bekir Çavuş approached me and said, "Sir, stop. This is unbecoming of you."

But I'd lost all control, determined as I was to beat Salih Ağa to within an inch of his life. Shoving Bekir Çavuş aside, I leapt forward again but some of the villagers surrounded Salih Ağa, preventing me from getting to him. In the meantime, the imam was muttering, "This is too much, far too much. I saw it, he attacked first."

Now nearly all of the villagers were standing in front of me, a half-circle of animosity, and more were coming as they heard the commotion, women and children alike. All those familiar faces seemed to be floating behind a nightmarish cloud. İsmail was standing there, hands impishly tucked into his sash, and the muhtar was looking at me, his gaze like that of a hungry jackal. A little farther away I could see Zeynep Kadın's head, which resembled a chunk of rounded stone, and beside her stood one of her daughters. All the while, small half-naked kids were crawling on the ground around my legs.

With a single lunge I managed to break through the circle of people surrounding Salih Ağa and just as I'd done when he was quarreling with Zeynep about her land, I grabbed him by the collar and shook him hard, but this time I threw him to the ground like a piece of rotten fruit and, just as I'd said I'd do, I ground him under my boot and started kicking him. Women were screaming, children were crying, and men were muttering to each other. I heard the imam exclaim, "This is a sin, a sin! God would never approve of this."

Others were shouting, "Grab him by the waist! Get his legs!"

But I was untouchable, clad as I was in the armor of my wild, unbounded fury. Suddenly, however, my attention was drawn to the consoling, soothing gaze of a friend, a caretaker, that glowed like the light of a single distant star in the darkness of night, the gaze of a lover . . . Parting the crowd, I began striding toward it.

*

That was the moment when I realized that something had changed in Emine's attitude concerning me. But in these days of hellish torment, I feel that I'm incapable of grasping the value of that moment. What's the value of a droplet of water dripping onto the face of a man who's been slung into a blazing fire? What's the value of the distant glow of lights for a man who finds himself lost in a desert in the middle of the night? What's the value of someone holding our hand as we writhe in pain while in the grips of an illness? What's the value of justice being served at the last minute for an innocent man who's being led to the gallows? What was the value of Mary Magdalene's tears as she wept at the foot of the cross upon which Jesus was crucified? When our eyes met, every sign of Emine's newfound feelings for me bore such incalculable value.

We had yet to speak. We had yet to spend any time with each other. I'd merely pass by, and she'd gaze at me. But our silent pact, our silent dialogues, bound us closer together than long, amorous conversations could ever do. Invisible tendrils that were stronger than steel stretched between us like a web that pulled us toward one another.

Once in the twilight of dusk I saw her at the fountain. She was alone. As silent as a shadow I approached her and said, "I need to talk to you. Somewhere secluded. Where can we meet? When?"

She bowed her head. But there was such submission in her posture, such surrender, that I could've easily taken her by the hand and led her to my house. I took a step closer.

"Tell me!" I said. "When, where?"

In a quivering, teary voice she replied, "Don't, please. They'll see us."

I'd heard her plead like that before. When I'd tried to catch hold of her as she bounded like an as yet unsullied, youthful deer by the stream in the copse of poplars near the village of [X], she'd always fled, the very same words on her lips.

But was she now saying it in the same tone of voice, with the same cadence? No . . . While the lyric was unchanged, the melody was new. It was now a thousand times more heartfelt and ardent.

When she'd said, "Don't, please" among the poplars, the overtone had been childish, coy, and naive. But when she spoke those very same words by the fountain, the meaning had shifted. "My will is weak," she seemed to be saying, concealing her fears: "Perhaps I won't be able to bear it and I'll give myself to you. I'd be disgraced in the eyes of everyone." My ears filled with the dizzying music of a woman whose flesh was voicing its desires.

"Don't, please. They'll see us . . ." Meaning: "I want this. I truly want this. But I'm afraid of what others will say." Such words are only spoken by people who share a secret.

"I don't want anyone to see us either," I said. "No one should know."

Shoulders tensed and head still bowed, she replied without looking at me, holding the now overflowing clay pitcher with one hand and clutching her sash with the other. "İsmail doesn't want me to talk to you," she said. "Leave me alone, please, leave me alone . . ."

She could've left. But she didn't, even though the pitcher was now full. More than anything, she wanted to complain to me about something, about someone. Water spilled out of the narrow mouth of the pitcher with a gurgle.

"Emine, I can see you're not happy. If you'd married me, I would've treated you with the greatest respect. I wouldn't have made you work like this, and I would've seen to all your needs."

Surprised, she looked up at me. Then she snatched up the pitcher, as though she'd suddenly remembered she had pressing matters to attend to.

"What's done is done," she said. "This is my fate."

Taking long strides, she walked off, and I stood there watching her.

*

Everyone promptly forgot about the catastrophe we'd suffered as if it had been nothing but a cloudburst. The overall atmosphere of the village, which had fluttered and rippled with the arrival of the enemy troops, quickly returned to its usual state of stagnancy. Once again the buzzing of swarms of flies filled the air as they flitted around mounds of filth, and occasionally the plaintive brays of my donkey cleft the silence as well, along with the wails of crying children.

There were no signs that we were situated so close to the rear lines of the hell, the apocalypse, that had burst forth and was raging to the west of the capital. Why hadn't the tithe collector come around as he always does before the turn of the season? Why weren't the gendarmerie tracking down conscripts? How had our village of [X] become a deserted island in the middle of the Haymana Plateau?

First I'd like to put those questions to these lands, as the villagers are unaware of the situation. When they realize something is amiss, they'll huddle together like penned animals, silently communicating with their heads and noses. For now they keep a distance, looking askance at me, the stranger, their enemy.

Their animosity reached new peaks after I beat Salih Ağa, and I constantly wonder if they might lynch me. Before, they'd left me alone, most likely because they knew I had a few guns, but when the enemy soldiers took them away, I lost all my power and prestige.

I can see it in their eyes.

Sometimes even İsmail, that crusty-eyed runt, glowers at me with such ferocity that I'm astonished.

The occupation of the village did nothing to unite us. If anything, the chasm between me and the villagers grew deeper, with a mere handful of exceptions. Bekir Çavuş has retained a certain sense of loyalty for the sake of his own interests. Emeti Kadın still deigns to work as my house servant out of sheer habit. And little Hasan, perhaps prompted by an unconscious sentiment, continues to respond to my overtures of friendship.

*

I've become so attached to Hasan that sometimes I go shepherding with him in the hills simply so we can spend time together. After packing my barracks bag with enough food for the two of us, I clip a large canteen of water to my belt and grab a long walking stick, and off we go in the early hours of the morning. The sunlight flickers and dances among the sparse, dry weeds. As I walk, I drift into daydreams while watching the play of light.

Like old travel companions, sometimes we amble together for hours without speaking a word, traversing roads and craggy passes. Once in a while we linger along the cool banks of streams and dig into our food as if we were having the finest of feasts.

Hasan has a habit of stretching out for a nap after we've had our fill, leaving me to watch over the herd. I sit observing the animals, watching how they come together and then drift apart again as they graze. Like the villagers and Hasan as he slumbers, I forget about the ring of fire around us that has transformed our lives. In the bosom of vast, blithe nature, I too become something vast and blithe.

Who cares about David Lloyd George? Or Raymond Poincaré? Of what significance are steel dreadnaughts, forty-two centimeter cannons, dumdum bullets, or hails of shrapnel? In the broad expanse of these rugged lands, how are the enemy soldiers any different from khaki-colored grasshoppers? The wind drives grasshoppers hither and yon. And what will be left are these stones, hills, herds, yellowed thistles, and stumps of willows, along with this little shepherd . . . And me.

Lulled by desolation and idleness, I slip into a state of numbness akin to being unconscious and lie back, resting my head on my arm. Hasan awakes and finds me asleep, or I wake up and see that he's still sleeping. The herd has either wandered off, or it's grazing next to us. Once I was stirred awake when a sheep brushed its moist muzzle against my face and another time a baby goat trod right across me. When they can't find anything to eat on the barren slopes, they rummage through the remnants of the food we brought.

Why has the invading army come to these lands, which can hardly support the small herd of a Turkish peasant? What could they possibly find?

*

One evening upon returning from one of my treks with Hasan, I found that the village was filled with enemy soldiers, inside and out. The squadron, however, was in complete disarray, unlike the troops who'd been here before. It was a chaotic swarm of people. If you add to that the overturned oxcarts, untethered mules wandering around, and trucks stuck near the top of a nearby hill, perhaps you can better envisage the kind of disorder that had broken out.

All of the soldiers were covered in dust, their faces had been sunburned a rusty brown, they had scraggly beards, and their uniforms were in tatters.

Despite the danger present in the situation, as well as the fear and bewilderment of the villagers, my heart leapt for joy, urging me to cry out, "So you lost, hah?!" But I never had the chance. As soon as we stepped into the village, I was surrounded by a group of soldiers, nearly all of whom spoke Turkish, and I was assailed by questions.

"Who are you? Where'd you just come from? What do you do? Where'd you get that canteen? Whose rucksack is that?"

Another group surrounded Hasan's herd. The villagers who had joined the crowd eyed us warily from a distance, ignoring our plight. As the circle of men closed in, brushing aside my replies, one of them pulled off my rucksack while another snatched the canteen from my belt. I gathered my wits when a third reached out for my jacket, shouting, "What do you think you're doing? Leave me be!" And with miraculous strength, I broke free.

The men, who moments earlier had been looking at me so viciously, suddenly laughed like a gang of tittering mischievous children. Spinning around, I glared at them, their laughter paining me more than the cruel look in their eyes. I stormed off, my chest aflame with fury as if my heart had been ignited with a burst of gunpowder.

By the time I got home after picking my way among soldiers sleeping on the ground and abandoned carts and beasts of burden, I was trembling with rage. All the same, now was the time for prudence, calculated action, and calm. The enemy had lost and was withdrawing in defeat. Nothing will remain of them but carcasses, trucks, gun carriages, and shreds of caps and boots, and the children of our villages will play with those trophies of victory like toys. These days, wouldn't doing anything except pulling back and waiting be sheer madness?

But I was infuriated. I grabbed a flowerpot from the windowsill and sent it crashing to the ground. Still enraged, I threw myself on the bed and started beating the mattress and tearing at it with my teeth. I was choking on the tears welling up within me but I refused to let them flow because I had just seen with my own eyes the triumph of the Turkish forces.

*

"Come quick! They're killing my boy!"

I leapt up and set off running with Emeti Kadın. When we found little Hasan on the side of the road, there wasn't an inch on his body that hadn't been beaten. The perpetrators, like the heroes of ancient Troy, were busy dividing up among themselves a now shepherd-less herd.

As I picked Hasan up, Emeti Kadın was tearing at her hair as she wailed, "Is he dead? Tell me, is he dead?"

I couldn't tell yet. He was bleeding from the nose and mouth, looking like a badly injured bird with a broken wing. I was trying to feel for the beating of his heart against my shoulder.

Gently I said, "Be quiet, Emeti Kadın, just be quiet . . . No, he's not dead."

But the poor woman didn't believe me. "He's dead!" she cried. "My dear boy is dead!"

I carried him to my house and laid him down in my bed. His grandmother, however, kept insisting on holding him in her arms.

"I'm a doctor," I said, "and I'm going to make sure he recovers. You need to just sit and calm down."

After soaking a few towels in water, I began cleaning the blood from his wounds. As I did so, the chill of the damp towels woke him. His eyes fluttered open and he glanced around in confusion. His eyes, which had always been like those of a frightened gazelle, now gleamed larger and moister than usual.

"See?" I said to Emeti Kadın. "He opened his eyes."

When I rubbed his temples and wrists with scented alcohol, he said feverishly, "Stop! It hurts." I then proceeded to gently touch various parts of his body, asking if it hurt, and he cried out in pain.

I decided to let him rest for a while. Emeti Kadın, who was now calmer, sat by the bed silently weeping. As I stood there looking at Hasan, concern flooding my heart, I became convinced that what had happened was a precursor to the calamities that were certain to befall us. "Those people," I said to myself, "will not leave until they've killed us all and burned down this village."

The night spread its wings outside my window like a bird of misfortune. It was too dark for me to see Hasan, who was still lying in my bed, but I could hear his labored breathing. After taking a quick breath he'd let out a sigh, and then the strained breathing would go on. As she sat in the corner, Emeti Kadın moaned incessantly. The room filled with the sound, as if someone was squeezing and releasing, squeezing and releasing, a rubber tube filled with air.

Out in the darkness I heard a commotion that seemed to be getting closer to my house. Before I even had time to think, "What's going on?" I heard the boom! boom! boom! of a fist banging on my door. Then a voice commanded, "Open the door, now!" After considering the available options, I said to myself, "Let them break it down if that's what they want." Soon enough the door flew open with a tremendous cracking and splintering followed by the thundering of feet, as though my home had been invaded by a roaming herd of animals.

Emeti Kadın murmured, "My God, they're coming! What should we do?"

I didn't have a chance to reply because the room was suddenly filled with soldiers shining electric lanterns around the room. One of them trained his light on my face while another found Hasan. Yet another peered around for Emeti Kadın, but when he couldn't find her, he set his lantern on my desk.

A voice said, "Up with you, light the lamp."

But I refused to budge. He grabbed my shoulder with a claw-like hand and shook me violently.

"I said, up! Light the lamp."

I don't know if it was because I glared at him with such deep hatred, but he let go.

Most likely terrified, Emeti Kadın whimpered, "It's on the sill."

The soldiers spun in the direction of her voice, shining their flashlights on her. Stunned by the light, she covered her face with her hands, whereupon the soldiers roared with laughter. Indeed, the sight was so bizarre that I almost laughed as well.

When they lit the lamp, I saw that there were six or seven soldiers. Two of them were low-ranking guards or officers, and I recognized a few of the others as the men who'd assailed me. Planting himself in front of me, one of them asked, "Got any weapons?"

"No. The others who came before you took them all."

Emeti Kadın added, "I swear, it's true. They took 'em all, just like he said. I saw it."

The same soldier asked, "Got any money?"

Pointing to a drawer, I replied, "I do. In there."

Pulling the key from my pocket, I tossed it toward him. All my money was there, rolled up. When he opened the drawer and placed the thick roll on my desk, Emeti Kadın's eyes widened. In the meantime, Hasan was trying to sit up but, too weak to hold up his own weight, he let his head sink back down on the pillow. All the while, however, he was looking at the men in the room with rapt attention.

One of the guards or officers asked, "Who's the kid?"

Emeti Kadın replied immediately, "My daughter's son. His father was a soldier like you. He got killed in the war."

Shrugging indifferently, he turned to me and asked, "Who's this woman?"

"She looks after me," I said.

The other soldiers were going through my room and, like last time, they started tossing my books onto the floor and poking into my belongings with their bayonets. I sat there observing them with collected coolness.

I did not, however, want them to get their hands on this notebook. Whenever they seemed to be reaching for it, my heart started racing. They rummaged through my wardrobe, trunk, and suitcases, throwing everything into a pile in the middle of the room.

In contrast to my calmness, Emeti Kadın was aghast at the sight of what they were doing, and I could tell she wanted to step in, say something, stop them somehow. I motioned for her to sit across from me. Again she sat, doubled over. All the while, Hasan appeared to be carefully watching everything, his dark eyes glistening.

Those eyes frightened me more than anything else. Those eyes *worried* me more than anything else. I thought that if I could only get closer to him, all my fears and concerns would vanish. Because of the noise in the room, I couldn't hear if he was still breathing. I considered calling out to him, "Hasan, Hasan . . ." But what if he didn't reply?

The soldiers were still hunting around in the room.

I said, "What do you want? You've taken everything already."

One of them replied, "We need something to carry this stuff in."

"Well," I said, "that's your business, not mine."

But they didn't need my help. A few of the soldiers took hold of the sheet on which Hasan was lying and pulled on it so quickly that, before I could say anything, the boy fell to the floor. The sound his body made on impact was that of a lifeless object: A dull thud.

Emeti Kadın and I dashed toward the bed. We tried to pick him up but his little body was heavy and stiff, and his back was wet with something slippery . . . I grabbed the lamp to take a closer look, and that's when I saw it. A small point between his shoulder blades. A small, black hole. What remained of his blood had flowed out from that hole, and the middle of the mattress was now covered in a large, dark stain.

I screamed so loudly it felt like my throat would be rent asunder: "You killed him. You killed him!"

They shoved me aside as if to say, "That's absurd." But when one of the men reared back in anger to punch me, he froze when he saw the body on the floor. Swearing left and right, the men left the room.

Their departure was, in essence, an escape. The corpse of a young shepherd had protected us from violence at the hands of the soldiers.

The corpse of a young shepherd . . . Emeti Kadın began wailing beside his body.

Such a sinister night! As if dawn would never come.

*

Morning broke. But what a morning! A morning of shrieks. Women cried out in lament and the weeping of children was punctuated by the howls of dogs. As though a ship was about to sink. As though a primitive orchestra was playing a mad composer's arrangement titled "The End of the World."

Neither Emeti Kadın nor I had slept as we waited for morning so we could bury Hasan. She wailed. I sat in silence.

By dawn, she was spent and her voice had given out. Her grief was now a deep rattling in her throat.

"Emeti Kadın," I said, "enough. Next they'll be coming for us. We're all going to share the same fate as Hasan." She raised her head from her knees.

"What are you saying?"

"I'm saying that they're going to kill us too. And before they leave, they're going to burn this village to the ground."

"Well let's run away somewhere then."

"What would be the point? I'm telling you, there won't be anything left of this place. Even if you do escape, you'll end up dying of hunger."

"Wait, what's that? I can smell smoke. Something's on fire."

I got up and closed Hasan's eyes. Never before had I seen a corpse that looked so alive. Though his eyes were now shut, a strange, disquieting gaze still peered out from between his lashes. Yet his expression was tranquil, as if he'd died without feeling any pain.

I'd seen that same look of serenity on nearly all the faces of the men I saw die in the Great War, their lips pulled into a relaxed smile, the smile of a man who's drifted off into a pleasant dream . . .

Perhaps death is the greatest of all physical pleasures. Perhaps, who knows? Soon enough I'll find out.

I covered little Hasan's face with a page from a newspaper because they hadn't left anything else behind, not even a scrap of worn-out felt or a dirty towel.

The screams coming from outside continued unabated, and some of the voices sounded familiar. I listened carefully. A man was shouting, "The fire's spreading to the mosque! Bring water, over here . . ."

That was the imam.

Another exclaimed, "The hayloft's on fire! Go that way!"

I recognized the voice as belonging to Bekir Çavuş. Then I heard the muhtar shout, "My woman's still inside! What should we do?"

"Now," I muttered to myself, "his crippled wife can finally die." In the distance I heard a woman who I thought was Zeynep Kadın scream, "Those pigs! Now they'll come here too."

I ran down to the door. As I was about to dash outside, I nearly ran into a strange, shapeless form that was somewhat human-like.

"Süleyman?"

In a weak voice like the buzzing of a gnat, he replied, "They burned down our place. If it's okay with you, I'll go lie down in a corner of the kitchen."

Wrapped in a filthy blanket, he was trembling, his twig-like legs barely supporting his frail frame.

"Go, go lie down. But it's not safe here either. Soon enough they'll come here too and set the place on fire."

As I was saying that, I remembered my notebook, so I went back up to my room, where I found it on my desk among some books, documents, and newspapers. After tucking it into my shirt against my chest, I paused, thinking that there was something else I needed. Of course, something to write with, as I knew I may never be able to return again. I found a pencil that had been whittled halfway down and slipped it into my pocket. Now I could leave, perhaps for the last time.

Using that stubby pencil, I'm going to record in this coverless notebook everything that happens to me until the final moments of my life. I will note here in the darkness of night all the mysteries surrounding this national catastrophe and ultimately leave these pages under a stone.

Any moment now—no, maybe two or three days later—the sound of marching Turkish boots will once again echo across these lands. And I'm certain that some of those soldiers will come here and carry out inspections of these wretched ruins. During that time, a swarthy private like Mehmet Ali will stumble upon this notebook and rush off to his commanding officer. Flashing a broad grin, he'll say, "Sir, sir, take a look at this. I wonder, what is it?"

The officer will slowly start flipping through the pages. As he gets closer to the end, his sense of curiosity will give way to excitement.

But I beseech whoever comes upon this notebook: Do not think that I bear feelings of ill will toward these people who treated me like a stranger and, not seeing me as one of their own, subjected me to incessant spiritual torment, for as I sat by the corpse of that little shepherd, I forgave them. As this calamity unfolds, I rescind all my grudges against them, even Salih Ağa, as they are unaware of what they have done.

If that is indeed the case, who is at fault? The fault is mine. And you, dear friend, reading these pages with such exhilaration, are at fault as well. For hundreds of years we left them, in the heart of this rugged nature, to be victims, suffering the deprivation of everything, of company with others, of all the pleasures of living. In their lives they have known nothing but hunger, illness, and isolation. And in that pitch dark known as ignorance, their souls have been held captive, as though imprisoned.

As regards love, compassion, and a sense of humanity, what could we expect of these poor people? The aridity of this climate has desiccated their souls. This solitude and isolation has taught them a brutal lesson in egoism, which is why they have become as beavers lurking in their dens.

*

After tucking my notebook into my shirt and slipping my pencil into my pocket, I stepped outside and started slowly walking in the direction of the flames, smoke, and screams.

All the villagers—men, women, and children alike—had gathered in the small square. The women were piling up what they'd been able to save from the fires and, once their work was done, they sat upon the heaps of their belongings and wept. Now that they realized it was pointless to struggle or resist, the men were standing around, their arms at their sides. I decided to approach them.

The behavior of the enemy soldiers surrounding us suggested they were eager to mock our plight. Some of them used their bayonets to frighten the women and children, while others took aim at people as if they were going to fire on them, whereupon cries would erupt from the crowd.

Occasionally soldiers would try to take things from the piles of possessions rescued from the flames. The women would respond with senseless pleas, saying, "We won't let you have nothing. Why don't you just take our lives . . . I won't let you have nothing. Ah, all we have left is our ruined lives, take those too." The immediate response was blows and kicks, followed by yet another eruption of screams.

One soldier planted himself in front of Zeynep Kadın and asked, "Why the angry looks? Because we took your gold, right? You have more. We know you do."

Zeynep Kadın replied, "You'll suffer for what you did, you pigs."

"Pigs? We're pigs? Well take this . . ."

And Zeynep Kadın fell under a rain of blows.

"What do we have here? Hey, why are you all covered up?"

That's what one infidel said as he approached Emine, who was cowering in terror, covered from head to toe, little more than a shapeless bundle. İsmail was standing with the men, watching the scene unfold from the corner of his eye.

"Uncover your face. Uncover it for me."

He had an Armenian accent. As he reached out toward her head, I approached one of the villagers and quietly asked, "Where are the soldiers' officers?"

"Don't know . . ."

I spotted Bekir Çavuş nearby, so I motioned him over.

"Don't these troops have any commanders?"

"Yes, they were here a little while ago. They're camped out over by the river."

"I'm going to go complain about what's going on here."

"Waste of time. They won't listen to you."

"No, I'm going to go."

I started making my way through the crowd in the direction Bekir Çavuş pointed out but quickly found myself surrounded by a few soldiers, who, by chance, didn't speak a word of Turkish. They said something in Greek, to which I responded in Turkish, but it was obvious nothing was being communicated, so I tried in French. Again they didn't understand. Using gestures and the few Greek words I could remember, I explained that I wanted to see their commanding officers. Maybe they thought that I'd said their commanders had summoned me, because they started to walk with me.

The officers were sitting in a makeshift tent, eating.

I approached them, still flanked by the soldiers. In French, I said, "If I may, I'd like to have a few words with you."

All four of them immediately got up and approached me.

One of them asked, "Who are you? And what business have you here?"

"As you can see, I am a cripple. And a veteran. I've retired to this village. I'm here to complain about how your troops are mistreating the residents of this village."

"In what way?"

"You burned the village down. You took all their food and money. But I don't see the point or necessity of further tormenting these poor people."

The officer furrowed his brow.

"Greek soldiers would never do such a thing. You must be mistaken."

"How could I be mistaken? I just saw it with my own eyes. And there's a shepherd boy lying dead at my home."

"Well, who knows what he did. We have the right to respond to the first signs of animosity with the most extreme measures. This is no game. We're at war."

"Indeed we are. I can understand burning down the village and taking our grain and money. But I'd like to repeat that tormenting women and children and subjecting them to abuse represents undue cruelty."

"Please. Weigh your words carefully."

As he was turning to leave and send me away, he stopped as though he'd remembered something.

"Wait," he said. "Please step this way."

Gesturing toward me, he said something to his friends in Greek.

"You're an officer, correct? Where and when?"

"In the Great War. I served on various fronts."

"Where did you lose your arm?"

"In the Battle of Gallipoli."

"Hah, so you must be a devout Kemalist."

"A Kemalist? Yes, but not because I served in the Gallipoli Campaign. Only because I'm an honorable Turk . . ."

The officers laughed.

"You're a more passionate patriot than we'd supposed."

Frowning, I looked down.

The officer added, "In that case, why aren't you on the other side of the battle lines?"

Again I said nothing.

"You probably thought we'd never get this far and so you didn't want to go to the trouble. But as you can see, here we are. If we'd wanted, we could've pressed on."

I maintained my silence.

"Were you thinking that was impossible? We could've kept pushing forward . . . But our aim here is not conquest. We're trying to secure peace. After all these years, aren't you tired of fighting? Is that all you Turks know how to do? Go to war? The entire world wants peace but you Kemalists insist on fighting."

One of the other officers said in rather poor French, "You'll come to your senses, but only after it's too late."

I said, "After you leave . . ."

"What was that? What did you say? After we leave? Haha, where are we going to go? The great countries of Europe sent us here to bring you to reason. Until we've carried out that humanitarian task, we're not going anywhere."

"Thank you very much. But were the atrocities you carried out in this burning village based on the orders of those 'great' countries you mention?"

The officer who'd first addressed me got to his feet and, after pulling on his hat, said, "Let's go see what these 'atrocities' are . . ."

As we walked toward the village, I walked in front and he followed behind. Once again I could hear the screams coming from the village square. I turned to the officer.

"It's always because of malice," he said to me. I was certain that when we reached the square, we'd come upon nothing that would justify such violent behavior.

In all truth, aside from little Hasan, no one else in the village had been killed or brought to grievous harm, and the actions of the soldiers hadn't gone beyond cruel taunting. All the same, their deeds pained me more and struck me as being graver than any massacre.

The officer, acting as though he was carrying out a serious inquest, questioned the villagers one by one through a soldier who spoke Turkish. Using the butt end of his whip, he pointed to the people with whom he wanted to speak, and then the questions began.

"What's your name? How old are you? Have you been beaten? Has anyone close to you been mistreated? Do you have any complaints?"

My blood began to boil when I heard the interpreter translating those rather peculiar questions. It was with great difficulty that I restrained myself from jumping in to answer them myself. And, based on the reactions of the officer, I could only surmise that the interpreter was twisting the meaning of the villagers' statements as he slowly translated them, which infuriated me to no end.

Walking up to the officer, I said, "This is a farce. When the villagers start speaking openly, the interpreter stops them with all kinds of threats. And I'm certain that much of what he's telling you doesn't correspond to what they're actually saying."

He contented himself with glaring at me. Turning to the soldier, he said something that was probably to the effect of, "Just ignore him," and went on with his absurd, vulgar game.

Some of the villagers could only stammer in response while others, thinking they were being clever, said they didn't have any complaints. For the most part the women merely broke down in tears.

Zeynep Kadın, however, didn't cry. The expression on her face, which reminds one of the wastelands of Central Anatolia, was sterner than usual, and her voice was like the howl of a female wolf.

"You burned down my house," she said. "You burned our wheat in the threshing fields. You took all our money and gold. You stole everything we have, down to my daughter-in-law's gold coin necklace. Now your men come along and want to take the blanket and mattress I'm sitting on. Pigs, pigs!"

The interpreter snapped, "Woman, mind what you say. If I tell the commander what you just said to me, it won't end well for you. Be sensible."

"And you, going on like that . . . After all this, what could I be scared of?" She then proceeded to pull down the front of her shirt, baring the top of her chest. "Go on, take my life! Take it!"

"Okay, okay. Just sit down," the interpreter muttered. "What a mess this is . . ."

But Zeynep Kadın was caught up in a fit of rage.

"We've lost everything, there's nothing left for us to eat or drink. So what's life worth? Now your men are going after our honor." She turned to her daughters and daughters-in-law and said, "Go on, say something!"

"Woman, shut your mouth!"

The interpreter was eager to move on and talk with someone else. Zeynep Kadın pointed to Emine and shouted, "Over and over your men tried to touch this poor girl!"

I was trembling from head to toe. Turning to the officer, I said, "If nothing else, this woman's state of agitation should say something to you."

Just then, Emeti Kadın appeared about a hundred paces up the road, doubled over as she struggled under the weight of Hasan's body, which she had hoisted onto her back. I ran toward her. When she saw me, she groaned, "Your house is burning too. They set it on fire. I barely managed to get him out in time." And then, like one of Shakespeare's witches, she toppled to the ground along with the dramatic burden she was carrying.

After laying Hasan out on the ground, I took her by the shoulders and helped her lean back against a wall.

"My God, the boy's so heavy! He wasn't like that before. I used to carry him for hours without a word of complaint. But now . . . I could hardly make it this far. My legs gave out. Go, your house is on fire!"

She was panting for breath as she spoke.

Hoping to save at least a few of my belongings, I ran to my house but it was too late. A thick cloud of smoke and tongues of flame enveloped the small building. There was nothing I could do. As I was about to go back to the square, I suddenly remembered my donkey. I kicked open the door of the barn, which had yet to be fully engulfed in the inferno, and found the donkey standing there, as unconcerned as ever, completely unaware of what was happening in the outside world. With some difficulty, I managed to nudge and shove it out of the barn.

And Süleyman? I yelled with all my might, "Süleyman! Süleyman!"

But there was no reply. Because of the smoke, my eyes were burning and watering, and my throat felt like it was clogged with tar. I shouted until my voice failed me. Stumbling like a drunk man, I made my way back to where I'd left Emeti Kadın and Hasan. She was sitting there, tearing at her hair. The body was gone.

"They took him, they took my boy," she moaned. "Where are they going to take him? What are they going to do with him? I would've run after them but I didn't have the strength."

"Emeti Kadın, I'll go find out."

I plunged back into the crowd in the square, asking left and right, "They took Hasan's body, did you see anything?"

All I got in reply were blank looks. "Which Hasan? What body?"

They'd lost all ability to comprehend, as if a void had opened up between their ears and minds . . . Nor was there any trace of the soldiers that had surrounded the villagers in the square.

Since I'd lost all hope of finding anything out about Hasan from the villagers, I set off in pursuit of the troops. When I found them, I went from soldier to soldier, asking in Turkish, French, and broken Greek if they knew anything concerning the whereabouts of Hasan's body. All of them, however, mocked my distress, and I was unable to get a direct answer.

Eventually I decided to huddle among the villagers in the square, as I was so ashamed that I didn't want Emeti Kadın to see me. Everyone was weighed down by their own concerns, asking questions like, "How are we going to find food?" As they hadn't eaten anything since the night before, the children were constantly crying. Taking Zeynep Kadın as an example, the old women sat around cursing about the existing state of affairs, while the young women and girls glanced around nervously, wide-eyed with fear. As for the men, they all sat together, and little by little they started to talk.

No one spoke with me. Even though we were sitting shoulder to shoulder, knee to knee, I may as well have been a hundred leagues away. With Emine, however, it was different, as though a secret bond of closeness stretched between us, and we glanced at each other from the corners of our eyes. But those brief, fleeting glances spoke volumes! Hers said, "Rescue me." Mine said, "Very well, I'm going to do just that." Hers said, "I've no one but you." Mine said, "You are the only person I think about."

Then we set about trying to find ways out of the conundrum in which we found ourselves. "Shall we run off?" "Yes, let's." "Where to?" "Just for a night." "But what if they catch us?" "They won't. Even if they do, I'll find a way out." "Yes, you will. You're the only person I believe in."

Human eyes have never spoken so elaborately. Set in the smooth skin of her face, her eyes were like a voice of flame . . . And that voice contained all the notes, all the melodies and harmonies, of an orchestra. It was as if all the heroines of grand music were passing before my eyes, writhing and crying out in their own particular anguish. From deep within a tragedy that reeked of the char of flames and human bones, I was reaching out to the symbols of this eternal calamity. And they all exist in Emine.

How gaunt her face was! As though the invisible hand of a master artisan had been hewing at her features for the last day, her cheeks were as sunken as those of a saint who, after years of fasting and tribulation, kneels in prayer before an image of Christ, afflicted with fever.

The noble shadow of a profound thought fell across her forehead, and her throat was as long as a swan's. I said to myself, *I'd like to bless the disaster that brought this transformation upon you.*

Two men sitting nearby were having a conversation. One of them said, "Not all of the grain in the threshing field burned up. I wonder if we could use it?"

"Probably has a burnt smell to it."

"I had an idea. What if we grind it after a good washing, and mix it with a little bran . . ."

"Wouldn't hurt to try. At least the kids'd get something in their guts."

All those concerns meant nothing to me! No longer do I have a stomach or guts. I'm a thought that has become fire consisting of naught but the spirit, emotion, and love, and I'm flying, flying, flying . . . And this tiny cluster of people surrounded by the ashes of this burned out village appear to me as a knot of ants on the edge of their crushed nest. Emine and I soar above them like complementary flames.

The two men beside me went on talking.

"They'll probably leave tonight . . . All of them have gathered down below on the plain."

"I saw them too. They loaded everything up and got their animals ready to go. A little while ago the commander was going to pitch his tent but didn't."

"What good would it do for them to stop? They'll go hungry, just like us."

"Real monsters though . . . They destroyed everything. Nothing left at all."

"Wonder if they did the same in the other villages?"

"What, you think if you went there they'd help you out?"

Another voice entered the conversation.

"Go see our Ağa here . . . Is he going to give you a single grain of wheat? Now, they didn't burn down his house. All his grain, hay, barley, and animals are there. He's nowhere to be seen, did you notice?"

"What'd he do to save himself?"

"There were those other soldiers who came through, remember? He was working with them. He got a paper from them, a document, whatever it's called. When he showed it to these people, they said, 'Take it easy, we won't do you any harm,' and they left him alone."

"Must be how it was with the imam too. He's nowhere around either."

"Last time he and Salih Ağa went with them, so . . ."

At any other time, I would've been infuriated by such talk, but now I was feeling completely indifferent. Let them do as they will. Let that miserable, wretched, impoverished crowd of people die of hunger, clutching their bellies. I've no need of food or drink. When darkness falls, I'm going to take Emine away with me, like how a wolf snatches a lamb from a herd of sheep. As soon as we're out of the village, we'll run toward our side of the front lines. If she grows weary, I'll carry her on my back. She looks so light, so very, very light, that I'm sure it'll be like carrying a bird.

It's now or never. The enemy soldiers will spend tonight having their way with the girls they'd been eyeing during the day. That's how the calamity they brought upon us will be brought to completion. It has to be that way, because no massacre would be complete without it.

In the course of wreaking devastation, people who have given themselves over to their bestial natures soothe those wicked desires they couldn't allay through torching and pillaging by forcibly possessing others, which, in the end, is the purest expression of animality. In any case, is murder any different? Spilling a man's blood and violating a woman's honor are more or less one and the same.

While at present I'm in the position of being the victim, I can still scrutinize the terrifying secret of these natural events in their dizzying savagery. Did I not mention that I now see everyone and everything from a different perspective? The abyss in humankind no longer sends me reeling because over time I've lost the sensitivity of civilized man. I'm no different than a creature that has slipped free of all social ties and been cast out of its den in these dry, barren lands among half-clad people. It is no longer possible for me, even for a moment, to transcend my instincts and rise up into the domain of general, abstract ideas. I can, however, hear the voice of my sexuality. In this clime of death and hunger, that voice is tantamount to all divine and rational truths.

Evening was falling. The propitious moment had arrived. Surrounded by the bandaged heads of men and women, I glanced at Emine as if to say, "Are you ready?" Earlier, the enemy troops had moved off into the distance to prepare for their departure, but now they were circling around us, cajoling the young women and trying to lure them away.

"Come, let me give you something to eat."

"Hey green eyes, look at me."

"Don't turn your head away. Are you angry? What did I ever do to you?"

"I won't ever let you go. I'll take you all the way to Athens."

"If you don't want to be with me, I'll take you to the commander. He'll give you money, food, and clothes. I can see you're barefoot. Wouldn't you like some beautiful shoes?"

Little by little, those taunts of the tongue became physical, and the poor young women found respite only by huddling together, gathering closer and closer until they became a large, single mass. Whenever a soldier reached out toward them or prodded one of the girls with the tip of his boot, they all screamed, which only whipped the troops into a greater frenzy.

"Here, take that. Now you can scream."

And those shrieks were harrowing.

One of the soldiers mocked the women with a vicious threat, saying, "We're going to pour fuel around you and set it alight, the same stuff we used to burn down your houses. You'll all be torched. But we don't want you all to die at once. In fact, we'd like to save the more beautiful women. So if any of you so desire, step forward now . . ."

His taunt was met with a silence that reeked of death. Until that point, İsmail had been standing there with his hands tucked into his sash, but his knees suddenly buckled and he fell to the ground. Zeynep Kadın croaked once again, "Pigs, pigs!"

She went on, "Hey pigs, what're these girls to you? Just leave them alone."

"Shut up, hag!"

"What did you say? What did you just say?"

And they started beating her.

I jumped up and said, "What do you think you're doing? You're going to kill the poor woman."

"Sit back down, this isn't any of your business."

A blow from the butt of a rifle sent me tumbling to the ground.

As twilight slowly settled over this tragedy like a sheer black curtain, people's faces started disappearing into the gloom, but when I turned my head to the side, I could still see Emine sitting four or five people away, looking at me.

While her features were indistinct and her face was as anonymous as a large flower in a garden at night, I could tell what she was trying to say. I decided to wait for it to get darker before venturing to move closer and speak with her.

But then there was another scream and all of a sudden one of our group was dragged away like a limb being torn from a body. A cloud of dust rose up as a commotion ensued near the place where Emine and her sisters-in-law were sitting. Snake-like I made my way behind the women and said as quietly as possible, "Emine, crawl backwards like me until we're behind the group of men. But go slowly . . . Yes, like that. Just like that."

Inch by inch she crawled backwards. The young woman they'd taken was one of Mehmet Ali's sisters. Her screams could be heard disappearing into the night. We started edging forward in the middle of the crowd of people. I whispered into Emine's ear, "Stay right beside me. Don't raise your head or your hips. Just keep crawling like this . . ."

I sensed that some of the villagers were leaning over to look at us, but everyone was so stricken with fear and bewilderment that they were in no state to pay attention to what anyone else was doing. Emine and I could've snuggled up there on the spot and no one would've cared.

Shoulder to shoulder we stopped to catch our breath. I listened to the sounds around us. After having sacrificed one of its own, the herd was quiet and still for a period of time. Even Zeynep Kadın had fallen silent. But soon enough the soldiers returned, again to the same point they'd been before, and the same half-threatening, half-teasing jibes continued.

"Why are you crying? Was that girl we took your sister? They're not going to do anything bad to her . . . If you'd like, come with me. I'll take you to her."

No one spoke a word. But the soldiers laughed—vile, ruthless laughter. Then there were murmurings, whispers. The terrified breathing of that mass of fifty or sixty people, and the night . . . How that night would end was a mystery.

I said to Emine, "Let's move a little farther off."

My mouth close to her ear, even more quietly I told her about my plan: "When we make it to the other side of the crowd, it'll be easy, as we can go to the cemetery and hide out there. But even once we're away from the others, we need to keep crawling."

Emine never replied but silently did as I said. The crowd, which stank like a herd of goats, didn't find anything strange about the way we were creeping along, whispering nose to nose like animals in a sheepfold, as if things had always been done that way. The only issue for me was that my left shoulder, the one that the soldier had struck with the butt of his rifle, was aching terribly.

"Emine, stop for a moment."

We were about to make our way out of the last circle of people but I was utterly exhausted and the pain was becoming unbearable. As if she could read my thoughts, Emine stayed put, not moving a muscle.

More cries filled the air as the soldiers moved in to take a second victim but this time men's voices were raised in the clamoring as well, and there was an uproar where we'd been sitting before. A scuffle, a quarrel . . . And then whips started cracking. The crowd surged forward and backward as if it was being pulled by opposing forces, and some people started running away.

"This is the time," I said to Emine. "Get up. Let's make a run for it too."

We ran, jumping over piles of rubble, toppled posts, carriage wheels, and yet more debris, and then we heard the whiz of bullets flying through the air.

"They're shooting at us!" Emine exclaimed and I clamped my hand over her mouth.

"Shh. We can hide behind that wall over there."

Leaping into the hot ashes of a house that was still on fire, we took shelter behind a mud-brick wall, the straw of which was still smoking. I could feel the pounding of Emine's heart as she leaned against me.

"Don't be so frightened," I said. "If you're scared, you won't be able to think straight."

The gunfire continued and the villagers were dashing in all directions, screaming as they ran. In the dark of night I heard the pounding of footsteps to our left and right, drawing nearer and fading away.

"Emine," I said, "one more time. Let's take the turn at your place and go up the hill, and we'll hide out in the cemetery."

Once again we started running. The soldiers were chasing after the fleeing villagers, madly firing volley after volley of bullets.

Emine suddenly staggered. "What's wrong?" I asked.

"I've been shot."

As she spoke those words, I felt a sudden pain in my right side. Gritting my teeth to conceal the pain, I took Emine by the hand and, half dragging and half carrying her, pressed forward.

I don't know how we made the turn in the road or climbed up the hill to the cemetery. But when we collapsed among the gravestones, neither of us had the strength to move another inch.

"I can't go on," she said.

"Where were you shot? Let me see."

She pointed to her left hip. I felt blood as soon as I ran my hand over it. And I could feel a trickle of blood running from my side all the way down to my foot. Unsure of what to do, I found myself gazing at Emine's face. Then it occurred to me to tear my outer shirt into strips that we could use for temporary bandages. With great difficulty I took off my jacket.

"Now take off my shirt," I said.

She held one end and I held the other, and we managed to tear it in half. After folding it lengthwise, we tied it around her, each of us holding one end.

Emine bolted upright and exclaimed, "What?! You've been shot too?"

Those words sent an unexpected surge of strength through me.

"It's nothing serious," I said. "A bullet must've grazed my side. It's only bleeding a little."

Emine reached out in the darkness with the compassion of a nurse.

True, she didn't know what to do. True, those hands were feeling around aimlessly on my body. True, they were not white and soft like the hands of an Istanbul gentlewoman, nor were they scented like lilacs. But those clumsy, calloused, bloodied hands reaching out from the earth toward me made me forget all my pain in that moment in which we were poised between life and death, and lent an ethereal pleasure to the fever now ravaging my body. Closing my eyes, I slipped into the waters of a cool dream.

In the dream, nothing remained of the tragic divide between the Turkish villager and the Turkish intellectual. Emine's arms, which were like the branches of a tree, were a stout, strong bond between me and that world of enmity and indifference. All of the repulsion, anger, wrath, and resistance that had led me to suffer hellish torments during the two or three years I spent in the village now began to flow out with the blood oozing from the wound in my side. As though an infection within me had ruptured and was draining out . . . I felt so at ease, like never before.

I said to Emine, "Let me just rest my head on your legs for a bit."

I'm not sure if İsmail's wife recoiled or not but without waiting for her to reply, I laid down on my stomach, placing my head on her legs.

The distant clamor of the massacre merged with the howl of the fever in my ears. I'm not sure how long it had been since I'd felt so tranquil and relaxed, but it seemed that my head, which was as hot as a witch's boiling cauldron, had only needed such a place to rest. Since all those years ago, yes all those years ago, when my mother's legs started to rot underground after she was buried, I'd never found a pillow so soft.

Emine folded up a piece of my shirt and placed it against my wound, and secured it in place by tying another piece around my torso. Then she draped my jacket over my back.

"I'm going to sleep a little and we'll set off toward dawn. Make sure you wake me up at daybreak."

Emine did as I said. But would I be able to get up? I pulled my notebook out from beneath my undershirt and took my pencil out of my pocket. These last few pages required a tremendous effort, made possible only by the superhuman strength afforded me by the fever brought on by malaria, but in the faint light of dawn I started to write.

I'd thought that after "write" I wouldn't have anything more to say. But it turned out that the real calamity was about to begin.

"Get up," I said to Emine.

But she couldn't. Her left leg was paralyzed. Poor girl, no matter how hard she tried, she couldn't get up.

"Can't move," she groaned. "Can't move."

*

Yet again I must journey forth. I will leave this notebook with Emine and set off alone, half-hungry, half-clothed, and, bleeding from my side, walk into the interminable distance stretching before me.

Glossary

Ağa: A local large landowner; used after a man's given name, it is an honorific for local notables.

Darbuka: A type of drum with an elongated body that is played with the hands.

Muhtar: The elected head of a village; local leader.

Şalvar: Trousers that are baggy in the legs and tapered at the ankles.

Zurna: A wooden double-reed wind instrument.